BARRY'S SISTER

BARRY'S SISTER

LOIS METZGER

Atheneum   1992   *New York*
Maxwell Macmillan Canada
Toronto
Maxwell Macmillan International
New York   Oxford   Singapore   Sydney

The author thanks Simon & Schuster for kind
permission to quote Dr. Oliver Sacks's essay "The
Disembodied Lady" from his book *The Man Who
Mistook His Wife for a Hat.*

The author also thanks Roz Chast for kind
permission to quote captions of two of
her drawings.

Copyright © 1992 by Lois Metzger

*All rights reserved. No part of this book may be reproduced or transmitted in
any form or by any means, electronic or mechanical, including photocopying,
recording, or by any information storage and retrieval system, without
permission in writing from the Publisher.*

Atheneum
Macmillan Publishing Company
866 Third Avenue
New York, NY 10022

Maxwell Macmillan Canada, Inc.
1200 Eglinton Avenue East
Suite 200
Don Mills, Ontario M3C 3N1

*Macmillan Publishing Company is part of the Maxwell Communication
Group of Companies.*

First edition
Printed in the United States of America
10 9 8 7 6 5 4 3 2 1
Book design by Kimberly M. Adlerman.

Library of Congress Cataloging-in-Publication Data

Metzger, Lois.
Barry's sister: a novel/by Lois Metzger.
p.   cm.
*Summary: Twelve-year-old Ellen's loathing for her new baby brother,
Barry, who has cerebral palsy, gradually changes to a fierce,
obsessive love, and she must find a proper balance for her life.*
ISBN 0-689-31521-X
*[1. Cerebral palsy—Fiction.   2. Physically handicapped—Fiction.
3. Brothers and sisters—Fiction.   4. Family life—Fiction.]*
I. Title.
PZ7.M5677Bar   1992
[Fic]—dc20   91-23738

*To Tony
and to the memory of my mother*

Acknowledgments

Heartfelt thanks to the following people and organizations: Robin Angel of United Cerebral Palsy of New York City, Inc.; Association for the Care of Children's Health; Leon Charash, M.D.; Roz Chast; Civilian Health and Medical Program of the Uniformed Services; Joanna Cole; Nancy Crampton; Eleanor Ebel; the Emerson family; Chris Gibson; Deborah Harvey, formerly of the Navy Wifeline Association; Tony Hiss; Susan P. Levine of the Family Resource Associates; Beth Lief; Judith A. Livingston, Esq.; Maureen Lynch; Thomas A. Moore, Esq.; National Information Center for Children and Youth with Disabilities; Lisa Pappanikou of the Sibling Information Network; Gail Paris; Robert E. Pasfield, formerly of United Cerebral Palsy Association of Nassau County, Inc.; the Pollack family; Fran Tortorelli, formerly of the Playground for All Children; Glenn M. Tracy, Lieutenant, United States Navy; Susan Wald, formerly of the Shield Institute; the Wawrzonek family; the Weitz family; and the Young Adult Institute.

Contents

PART ONE

The Forever Bug

CHAPTER

1

New and improved—that's how I was feeling that Friday afternoon in September three years ago. Like a big box of detergent with better whiteners and softer fabric softener and double-strength static control. Presenting Ellen Gray, now with Patience, Tolerance, and Understanding, and a full money-back guarantee.

My mother was a half hour late getting home from work, and ordinarily I got all edgy about this kind of thing. Now, at the kitchen table, drinking milk and taking apart Big Stuf Oreo cookies, I was practicing patient, tolerant, and understanding greetings. To take the place of my usual "Why are you so late!" would be "I'm so sorry you were delayed," or "Poor Mom. You must be exhausted." And "Would you like a nap? *I'll* make dinner." This was surprisingly easy. My plan was that I would be packed with improvements by the time my father went away again in January.

But I didn't want to think about that yet.

Anyway there were too many good things to think about. Two weeks before, I'd made my junior high school softball team, even though I was only a brand-new seventh-grader. Just that afternoon, even though we lost a game we should have won, I'd hit a single and a double and, playing third base, had made the long throw and nailed three runners at first. Afterward the girl playing first, an eighth-grader named Roz Spinak, who was shy and awkward and barely ever spoke to anybody, told me, "You've got a great arm." Best of all, Ms. Moore, our coach, who supposedly never complimented anybody unless maybe she hit a grand slam in the bottom of the ninth, muttered in my direction, "Ellen Gray, you're about to start improving." I'd felt my whole self fill up, as if I'd been named Most Valuable Player at Peter Minuit Junior High.

Cool, pale yellow light washed over the yellow walls of our kitchen. I peeled apart six cookies without breaking any. Was there anything I couldn't do? Bells jingled down the stairs in the hall, bells attached to the collars of two Labrador retrievers who lived up on the fifth floor. Their toenails clicked on the tiles; their breathing was heavy and slightly wheezy. The black one was named George, and the yellow one, Gracie. I live two floors down from George and Gracie, in a loft in Soho, way downtown in Manhattan in New York City.

"Hello, dogs!" I heard my mother's voice out in the hall. I sat there happily, anticipating her shock at encountering so much patience. But she never even noticed it. Her first words to me, pouring out all in a rush, were, "Do you have any idea how I feel?"

I shook my head, disappointed. So then I practiced understanding, telling myself that my mother often plunged into conversations, the same way she plunged into cold swimming pools. She wasn't the type to dangle her feet on the edge and say, "It's freezing. I'll get used to it this way first." That type was my Aunt Beryl, my mother's sister.

"So, how do you feel?" I asked her. One thing I had to notice—she looked terrific. Her gray-blue eyes were all bright and alive, her cheeks rosy and flushed. She had a way of blushing that people found charming. I usually blushed a sickly scarlet that led people to ask if I was "feverish."

"I have a strange metallic taste in the back of my throat," my mother said, sitting down beside me on one of our high wooden chairs. "And there's a hollow, heavy feeling in my chest—the way the air feels when it's about to rain."

"What'd you have for lunch?"

"Chicken salad on rye, and it had nothing to do with this." She smiled, exposing perfect teeth. If there was anything about my mother I envied, it was her teeth. I'd worn braces when I was younger, nine and ten, and had barely recovered from the moment a tiny rubber band popped out of my mouth and landed right on Faye Needleman's looseleaf.

My mother said, "Aren't you going to ask why I feel this way inside?"

Sunlight played on her shoulder-length, light blond hair. I finally caught on. My mother had news, and this was her way of introducing it. A year and a half earlier, when my father, an officer on a submarine, was going to live at home nonstop for two whole years, something he'd never done before in my entire life, she'd asked me, "Aren't you wondering why I bought a new cushion for the rocking chair?"

So if a new rocking chair cushion meant my father was going to be home for two years, what news was she telling me now?

"Is Aunt Beryl getting remarried?" I said.

My mother tightened her lips, trying not to laugh. "The

5

first marriage was disastrous enough," she said. "Poor Beryl. Guess again."

I thought of my grandparents. The reason we'd moved to New York six and a half years ago was to keep a closer eye on them. "Are Grandmother Anne and Grandfather Mitchell leaving the residential home and coming here to live with us?"

"God forbid! One more try, Ellen."

I shut my eyes a moment, praying hard I was right this time. "Is Daddy staying home for good?"

My mother's shoulders sagged a bit. "No, honey, Dad's got to go back to sea in only a few months."

"I give up!" A cramp pinched my neck. Maybe there was something else about my mother I envied. She always handled it so well, when my father went away. Besides, why were we playing Twenty Questions? Didn't she care that her only child was newly improved?

"I'm pregnant," my mother said. I stared at her. "Three months already, El. I didn't want to tell you sooner, because the first three months are kind of tricky . . . there might be danger of a miscarriage. And I didn't want you to be disappointed after getting all excited."

Excited? But I felt the exact opposite of excitement. In six months—March, almost springtime—a new Gray baby. That didn't sound right. My mother picked up an Oreo I'd skillfully taken apart, put it back together, and ate it. She was giving that new Gray baby *my* cookies!

"How does it feel, Big Sister?" she asked me.

I moaned to myself. "It feels like . . . I'm a pain in the neck—I mean, I have a pain in my neck."

That made her laugh. I had to laugh too so it would look as though I didn't care that I'd said something so silly. So why wasn't I excited about this new baby? Lots of kids

6

at school adored their younger brothers and sisters, and idolized their older ones. Last year, in sixth grade, Susie Brockleman bragged for weeks that her mother was going to have a baby boy.

George and Gracie came back upstairs, wheezing more heavily than ever. But now the bells and the clicking of their toenails sounded far away, too far to reach. Of course, if I ran out to the hall, I'd get two slurpy tongues and hot musty breath in my face, and two tails playfully thrashing my legs. But I didn't move from my chair.

"Why'd you get home so late!" I burst out suddenly. So much for patience and those other things.

At dinner that night, my mother said, "I've told Ellen." I had to admit, my mother looked lovely. She has a face designed for laughter, full of laugh lines and dimples. "Now Ellen knows."

"Wonderful," my father said. "Isn't it funny—now the baby seems more real."

I sat there, rubbing my neck. I must have pulled something during those heroic throws to first. I observed them both with cranky suspicion, as they ate two plates of spaghetti apiece while I could barely eat one. "So when are you leaving, exactly?" I asked my father.

"January third," my father answered crisply. He'd been a navy career man for thirteen years, and I couldn't remember a moment when he didn't seem alert and eager.

"When's the new Gray baby due?" I said. "March, right? You'll be away, won't you?" My voice cracked a little on the word *away*.

"I plan to be back in March," my father said, his light, light blue eyes fixed on me. When I was little I called his eyes "blue ice."

"Briefly," I said with emphasis. "You'll be back only briefly. Aunt Beryl says you'll be away for the next three years." I began to get a funny feeling in my stomach, as if some weird machine was plugged in and starting to hum. Something told me this machine had better get turned off, and fast.

"Aunt Beryl, as usual, doesn't know what she's talking about," my mother said. "Dad will be on patrol at sea for two months, and then home with us for almost a whole month, and then nearby up in Connecticut for about a month, getting ready to go back to sea. Then the four-month schedule will begin again, and will keep on repeating itself, for three years. After that he'll be on shore duty in Connecticut for another two years. The navy knows their people would go nuts without those long spells ashore. Besides, anytime Dad's in Connecticut, he can call, and visit on weekends. We'll be seeing lots and lots of Dad."

I knew that wasn't exactly true. My strongest memories of my childhood, which started in Connecticut, and then moved to New York when I was five, had to do with Daddy being "away." The word has always sounded endless to me, like the space beyond the sky. "Maybe Daddy started something he can't finish," I said. "Like he planted a seed in the ground and then left the gardening for somebody else."

That got my mother angry. She said that my father was one of the most responsible men she'd ever met; she said he was a wonderful, kind man; she said he'd done a fine job of raising me up even though he was away a lot. What she didn't say was that in a way I was right.

"I'm sorry," I said. "I'm not in the greatest mood. We lost today in softball, playing a school that's practically in last place."

"Too bad," my father said, smiling, placing a warm, slightly damp hand on my arm. If he was mad at me too, he wasn't showing it. I liked his hand on my arm, and his blue-ice eyes, and his smell of strong black coffee, which he drank all day, and the tiny, tiny chip off his front tooth that he said only I had ever noticed, not even my mother. The kitchen was dark now, and I could hear cars and trucks rumbling by on the cobblestone street below. This was the perfect moment to brag about my own performance at softball, but Ms. Moore's words—"about to start improving"—suddenly seemed so meaningless.

My father leaned over and felt my forehead. "I think Ellen's got a touch of sibling rivalry fever," he said.

"She's eleven," my mother said.

"Eleven *and a half*," I corrected her.

"Then it's worse than I thought. Eleven and a half, and a year ahead in school. You're much too old and too smart for that. But you've got your liver in a quiver about something, that's for sure."

Sibling rivalry fever. I wondered how long that would last. Twenty-four hours, or forty-eight hours, like a bug?

My mother was still a little mad at me when I went to bed, but then she woke me up later to watch a comedienne making her first appearance on the "Tonight Show." My mother did that sometimes. We sat on the soft living room couch, laughing at jokes about the comedienne's weird relatives. My mother's cool, slender arm was wrapped around me, and I could smell her slightly rosy, soapy smell. Behind the TV, through the large windows of our loft, I saw the flat gray top of the supermarket across the street and, next to that, a tall apartment building with a cast-iron front. On the other side of the apartment building was a small vacant lot. A year before, it had been a coffee shop. Soho was full

9

of crowded streets, but then there were these empty spaces, like the vacant lot and the back alley just outside my bedroom window, where I could hear real alley cats yowling and scuffling. Looking up, I saw a bright purple-blue sky. New York City never gets completely dark. It's one of the things I've always liked—just like the smell of soap or roses. Was I going to have to share all this with an outsider, who was already sitting right next to me?

CHAPTER

2

In softball I fell into a slump . . . that lasted and lasted and lasted. Balls scooted right by me as if they had an important appointment way out in left field. The few times I managed to catch one, I threw it so badly to first that Roz Spinak had to scramble for it. At bat, I mostly popped up or struck out. Ms. Moore, who is tiny, four foot ten, but tough as a sumo wrestler, returned to her more customary smirking, shaking her head at me. Once, on the bench when our team was at bat, she grumbled, "I don't know about you, Ellen Gray." Well, that made two of us.

We played our last game on a cool November afternoon, and Central Park looked stunning—maple and oak trees were soaked in reds and yellows, and thin lines of clouds spread out across the sky. It almost made me forget that my twenty-four-hour bug hadn't ended in twenty-four hours, or in forty-eight, or even in seventy-two. Was it turning into a Forever Bug?

We won, no thanks to me. Ms. Moore announced that we ranked twenty-fourth out of seventy junior high school softball teams. Several people clapped; several moaned. "Yes, you should moan!" snapped Ms. Moore. And so ended the season.

Roz and I picked up the bases and carried them off the field to the subway, to bring them back to school. Other kids took bats and balls, minus one ball that a senior had smacked into the bushes and that completely disappeared.

"You'll definitely do a lot better in the spring," Roz said. "Not that you definitely didn't do well this fall."

"Two pop-ups and a strikeout in this game alone," I said easily, letting her know it was okay to talk to me. "Then I finally hit the ball—right into a double play!"

"It's a slump," Roz said, carefully. "That's all."

"A slump," I said. "My whole life is a slump!"

Her eyes brightened a moment. She had light brown, almond-shaped eyes. "Bad players can get lucky and smack the ball for a base hit every time," she said. "It's when you're really good that you start making good-player mistakes, like striking out and popping up."

I had to smile. "That's a new way to look at it," I said. Roz was pretty, in a kind of hidden way—you had to observe her closely before realizing that her slightly large jaw, broad nose, pudgy cheeks, and thick, blunt cut, nearly black, chin-length hair all fit together in a way that actually made her appealing. Roz also had smooth, glowing, clear skin— the kind of skin that made me think, That's how skin ought to look.

"Who do you have this year?" she asked me, as we waited for the train. "I probably know most of your teachers from last year."

I rattled them off for her. When I got to English, mostly taught by substitutes, I remembered something one of them had spent a whole class on, even though everyone

12

except me was yawning or groaning throughout. It was about the three Brontë sisters, including Emily, who wrote *Wuthering Heights*, and Charlotte, who wrote *Jane Eyre*. "When they were all very young," I said, "they gave their only brother some toy wooden soldiers. They all started playing together, and suddenly it was more like the girls had given this gift to themselves. In a great big creative burst, all the sisters started writing stories, tiny script on tiny pieces of paper. Toy wooden soldiers, that's what it took."

"I believe it," Roz said. "Everything can click, if you're ready for that to happen."

So, she hadn't yawned or groaned, either. Warmth spread through me, as if I were curled up in front of a fireplace. It made me think that while I was friendly with lots of kids at school, kids I'd known way back in kindergarten, even, I'd never had a real, true-blue best friend.

Then we got back to teachers, and at the end of my list was Ms. Stapler, for speech and homeroom. Roz shuddered, and said, "Oh, *her*. She's not my favorite human being, I can tell you that." After a moment of silence she yanked down her shirt, and said, "Ms. Stapler's going to make you get up and deliver a five-minute speech to the class. It's horrifying."

I shrugged. "It doesn't sound so bad. I'll practice in front of the mirror and stuff."

"It's scarier than you think. At least it was for me. Ms. Stapler kept interrupting with all these questions." More moments of silence. I was realizing that Roz was different, complicated, in a way I liked, when she gave another yank to her shirt and said, "Anyway, that's not why I don't like Ms. Stapler. My mother died last year, and Ms. Stapler clapped her hands for silence and then told the whole class that Roz Spinak would be sad for a while. The way she said it, it sounded just like an announcement for a special assembly in seventh period!"

I began squirming around, shifting my weight from foot to foot. "Uh-huh," I said. The trouble was, I wasn't too crazy about anything . . . tragic, and always tried to avoid it, like poison ivy, so it wouldn't leave a rash. My mother's parents died in a car crash when my mother was only seventeen. She rarely talked about it, but when she did, it made me want to put my hands over my ears and hum. I didn't want to feel that way now. I wanted to show Roz how understanding I could be. But somehow I got to thinking about how, only a week before, my father's tour of duty at a naval recruiting center in the World Trade Center had ended, and he was already spending a lot more time in Connecticut, getting ready for his next patrol. Daddy—away. It felt like a fist closing over my throat.

"Are you definitely all right?" Roz said. Even with some of her old shyness creeping back, she was the understanding one.

"Fine," I said, from the back of my throat. I felt chilly all of a sudden, and pressed the dusty bases to my stomach. "Actually, no, I'm not fine. I pulled a muscle—in my arm. Listen, I'm really sorry about your, uh, mother." I actually almost said, "dead parent." How crude!

"I didn't tell you that to get your sympathy," Roz said, smiling. "Looking back, it's kind of funny. Ms. Stapler, so proud of herself for being so concerned, when really she was so heartless. Horrible-funny, you know what I mean?"

"Uh-huh," I said. Then the train pulled in, and it was so noisy we could barely talk. But we still didn't talk much even after we got off. As we unloaded the equipment at school, Roz asked me, "You want to get together sometime? See a movie or something? It definitely doesn't have to be a movie."

"Sure," I said. "A movie, or something that's not a movie." What was wrong with me? A dead parent wasn't contagious! Still, whenever I saw Roz in the halls, we talked a little, but it just never clicked again, not like before.

The holidays came and went, and I was happy to see them go. My whole family, small as it was, gathered in a noisy cluster around our tiny Christmas tree in the living room and talked nonstop about the baby, the baby, the baby.

Grandfather Mitchell proudly showed us pictures of a crib he'd ordered from a catalog, plus sheets and blankets and even a washable wool mattress pad—behind Grandmother Anne's back, I gathered, because she kept saying how surprised *she* was, and wasn't *he* the extravagant one! Aunt Beryl said the pitter-patter of little feet would be music to everybody's ears.

I got a bunch of boring, generic gifts—a check for ten dollars, a couple of scarves, a muddy-colored wool vest. The new Gray baby was already getting better presents than me.

January 3—the day my father had to go away. I was surprised to find it an ordinary day, like a lot of others. We woke up; the sky was white with clouds; we ate Spoon Size Shredded Wheat. There's a bakery down below, in the next building, and some mornings the smells come in through our windows. It can smell like hot, fresh baked bread, or like prune Danishes, or, as it did that day, like a cake made entirely of frosting. But my stomach was jumping all around.

"I'll see you in less than nine weeks," my father said. Of course my father used to go away constantly, until only a couple of years before, but when I tried telling this to my stomach it wouldn't listen. My father smoothed the hair off my forehead, and carefully gave me a soft, warm kiss. "I'll be thinking of you, Ellen," he said.

When I was little, I always begged him to write me or call me, though I already knew better even then. A submarine listens all the time, for incoming messages in code, but a submarine won't transmit messages ever, not for any reason unless it's a distress call when there's a horrible disaster, because any signal would give away its position.

"I'll be thinking of you too." I was holding my stomach. My mother, whose own stomach was now alarmingly big, was crying softly. But I knew she'd finish all her crying tonight, getting over it by tomorrow morning. How long would it take for my stomach to get over this?

The following weekend, Aunt Beryl invited herself to sleep over—"to cheer up the lonely gals," as she put it. I'd almost forgotten that she slept over a lot when my father was away. It always put me on the living room couch for the night, because Aunt Beryl couldn't sleep in the living room—she said our big windows made the room "much too exposed."

Aunt Beryl drove over from her house in New Jersey, and when she arrived that Saturday night, clutching a gray overnight bag, carrying a long, dark-plum down coat, wearing a straight brown skirt and a peach blouse with billowing shoulder pads, she stood in our doorway and announced, "I am half dead."

I'd heard that before, and also, "I am completely dead," and simply, "I am dead." Usually she blamed her business for her deceased state—she did some kind of consulting work I never quite understood—but tonight it was the traffic, she said, and somebody stole a parking space from right under her nose, and now her car had to be stored in a garage overnight, costing her nearly a month's mortgage payment.

Actually she did look exhausted. "Aunt Beryl," I said, "would you like to rest and put your feet up?"

"Oh, no! Then the blood would rush to my head and I'd feel faint."

My mother couldn't help laughing. "Beryl, Ellen wasn't suggesting you hang upside down!"

"If it's all the same to you," Aunt Beryl said, "I'll just sit."

Plopping down on the couch, Aunt Beryl slipped off her low-heeled brown shoes, and said, "I've got a pebble in my panty hose. It's killing me. However did a pebble get inside there? Oh, look, it's caused a run." Rubbing her feet, she managed to pick out the pebble. "Now will you look at that! It's *tiny*. How could anything so tiny hurt so much?"

"It's always the tiny things that hurt the most," I said. "Like needles, for instance. And bee stings, and deadly poison darts."

Aunt Beryl scrunched up her face. "Ellen's morbid," she told my mother. "Loretta, why is Ellen so morbid?"

"She takes after you," my mother said, winking to let me know she didn't mean it for a minute.

Unfortunately for Aunt Beryl, she didn't resemble my mother. She had short, curly, reddish hair, and eyes so small you had to know in advance they were hazel. She

17

looked my mother up and down, up and down. "Loretta, do you miss your skinny little waist?" she said.

"Not at all," my mother replied, giving her belly a pat. As she went into the kitchen to check up on the meat loaf, Aunt Beryl's favorite dish, I could tell she was far too happy to let Aunt Beryl get under her skin.

"What about you, Ellen?" Aunt Beryl said. "Do you miss your daddy?"

I swallowed hard. "Sure," I said. My mother had once told me she'd never loved any man before falling in love with my father instantly, the moment she met him. I believed her. He was so big and strong and solid, as if there were a redwood tree growing inside him.

"My husband was always going off too," Aunt Beryl said with a mournful sigh. Aunt Beryl had been married to a dentist for two years. Her divorce came through when I was still a baby. "He neglected me so utterly that I could never marry anybody else ever again," she said years later. My mother once told me that after their parents died, it was Beryl who ended up taking care of Loretta, even though Beryl was only two years older. "I was such a mess, Ellen, you have no idea," my mother said. "It was Beryl who made sure I ate three meals a day." When Beryl married the dentist she told my mother, "Now, at long last, somebody will take care of me!" It made me feel bad for Aunt Beryl, that it hadn't worked out that way.

Now Aunt Beryl said, "Men are always running off and disappearing, as if it were part of their job."

"It is part of Daddy's job!" I said. "That's what his boat does—swims out into the ocean somewhere and disappears, so that no enemy submarines can ever find him. And he has to stay disappeared for two whole months."

Aunt Beryl wiggled her toes. "Some kinds of disappearing are more permanent than others," she said.

I felt the blood leave my face. Secret, secret, I remembered from a long time ago. Where is Daddy? I cried. Where did Daddy go? It's secret, Mommy said, secret. Daddy's not allowed to tell. Even Daddy doesn't know where he's going, until he's actually on his boat and told to go someplace. Why, Mommy, why can't I know where Daddy is? Is Daddy on the bottom of the ocean, where it's dark and cold? Is he spinning around like seaweed? Can he breathe at all? Don't cry, honey, the air is wonderfully mild and fresh on a submarine, and Daddy says you'd never even know you were under water, that it's like being in a narrow room with no windows, which tilts every so often. That's not so scary, is it?

"He's coming home in March," I said slowly.

"Of course he is!" Aunt Beryl stretched her lips apart. It took me a moment to recognize it as a smile. "All I'm saying is that my husband was always going away too, to meetings and dental conventions and whatnot."

"But that's different," I said.

"It's always *different*," Aunt Beryl said. "Isn't it?"

My mother often warned me not to listen to Aunt Beryl too carefully. But I couldn't stop Aunt Beryl's words from traveling right past my head and my heart—right for my blood, to shoot around my system.

"I'm trying to open your eyes," Aunt Beryl explained. "Things happen. People disappear."

My mother called out, "Dinner's ready!"

After only a few bites, the meat loaf sprouted wings inside me and flew around. Images flooded my brain. My father, his submarine crushed and broken, lying on the black, airless, silent ocean floor, where the tremendous pressure caused fish to look weird and monstrous. Aunt Beryl talked on and on about a client who owed her seventeen hundred dollars. What did people consult her about, I wondered, and actually pay her for? Why did she appoint herself my consultant, for free?

That night, on the living room couch, I stared out at a huge, gleaming, nearly full moon behind feathery clouds.

Things happen. People disappear.

Now my father was away, and I had flying meat loaf in my stomach. Why did things have to just happen? Why change them at all, if they're basically all right to begin with? I knew this was the baby's doing, somehow. The new Gray baby started this. That baby was ruining everything.

In speech class, Ms. Stapler's favorite word was "unacceptable." When it came to my thoughts and feelings about the new Gray baby, I also kept hearing her word in my head. Unacceptable. But was there a way to turn off thoughts and feelings as easily as turning off a faucet?

As it turned out, yes, there was. You could create a quiet, still, empty space inside yourself, taking up room the way pieces of insulating foam fill up cracks around windows so that icy cold air can't get in. I called it "the Calm." It was far better than Patience, Tolerance, and Understanding— my whole body relaxed, even my stomach. At school, I watched the other kids as if I weren't one of them, but a scientist, maybe, studying twentieth-century junior high school behavior. Girl chewing ravioli with mouth wide open; never learned manners. Boy smiling with tightly closed lips; embarrassed about protruding buck teeth. Two girls fiercely arguing over boring boy who wasn't near worth it. Many kids looked completely wild to me, acting up in class and throwing chairs in homeroom, as if leaving elementary school automatically turned them into maniacs.

The Calm became my talent. I got so good at it that when my mother told me she'd completely forgotten my birthday (February 2, also known as Groundhog Day) and, not only that, had arranged for us to spend the night in New Jersey at Aunt Beryl's, I said simply, "No problem."

"I'm so sorry," my mother said, her eyes as meltingly sad as a cocker spaniel's. "I didn't even get you a present! I'll make it up to you, El, I promise. I'm not myself these days."

Then who are you? I thought, but just looked at her.

"I don't want to break our date with Beryl and disappoint her. She's had so many disappointments."

"Fine," I said. "No problem."

My mother frowned. "Since when did that expression become number one on your hit parade?"

I shrugged. "Since my eyes got opened," I replied.

"I'll let that one go by," my mother said. But she was still frowning.

Aunt Beryl cooked macaroni and cheese, and baked an angel food cake. The Calm impressed her. While sipping steaming, minty Sleepy-Time tea in her overly warm dining room, surrounded by dark burgundy curtains that looked black at night, Aunt Beryl told my mother approvingly, "Ellen is maturing, finally."

I inhaled deeply, feeling complimented. I had accomplished something, after all.

"But Ellen has lots more years to be a kid and have lots of fun," my mother said. "Don't mature too fast, El."

"Nonsense," Aunt Beryl said, taking a long sip. "The sooner, the better. You never know when you'll have to mature overnight."

"Aunt Beryl is right." I took a long sip to emphasize my agreement, even though it burned the roof of my mouth. "If you act like a little baby who needs her mommy and daddy, it's only worse when things happen and they disappear."

"Who's disappearing?" my mother said, frowning again.

She's going to get permanent frown lines on her forehead, I thought, right over her laugh lines. "You don't always have to leave," I said. "You can be in the same room, even, and still disappear." I quickly added, "But that's no problem!"

Outside, it was cold enough to freeze your lips to your teeth. As we finished our tea in silence, a chill swept through Aunt Beryl's steam-heated house.

My mother was placed in "the guest room," as Aunt Beryl called it, and I ended up in "the sewing room"—a narrow, coffin-shaped area that smelled of piles of old clothes, with a tiny window that looked out on a weedy vacant lot. My face, on the flattest, most lifeless pillow in the world, was only inches away from Aunt Beryl's sewing machine, its needle in midair. The needle scared me. Suddenly, in one mind-crushing moment, in less time than it takes to actually think, I prayed, Please God, make something happen so that the baby will disappear.

I tried burying my face inside the pillow, but could only sort of fold it around my head. There was no hiding it anymore. I was messed up, about as messed up as a person could ever get. Wishing a little tiny baby would die! It even made me feel sorry for it. The new Gray baby had no idea it was entering a world with a big sister like me in it.

3

*Roz Spinak had warned me—Ms. Stapler as-*signed a five-minute speech, on any topic, as long as two kids didn't pick the same one. Not too likely in my case. Who else was going to do "Robert Gray, Department Head Aboard a Fleet Ballistic Missile Nuclear Submarine"? It turned out two kids did want to do Madonna, but neither of them got it, because Ms. Stapler called the topic "unacceptable."

I wrote out key phrases about my father on three-by-five cards, and practiced my speech in front of the mirror over my bureau until it sat as comfortably in my head as old furniture in a room.

The first card: *Little boy.* I gazed at my own reflection, treating the girl with longish, wavy brown hair and grayish eyes who stared back at me as if she were simply one of many enraptured listeners. "When my father was a little boy," I began, "he owned a book that had a yellow cover and blue-and-white drawings. This book was all about the atom." I turned slightly, to tell this to the lamp in the shape of a duck on my night table.

"Protons, neutrons, and electrons were characters in the book. They introduced themselves to the reader, saying things like, 'Hi, I'm Mister Proton!' Silly as it sounds, my father got hooked, and read everything about the atom he could get his hands on. It absolutely fascinated him, knowing that atoms existed, but that nobody could ever see them. You can see where atoms have been, because they leave tracks, and you can see the electrical and magnetic fields surrounding atoms. But even the most powerful microscopes can only see molecules, which are made up of great numbers of atoms.

"So," I went on, glancing knowingly at my desk and wooden chair, "my father knew from a very young age that his whole life would revolve around the atom. Eventually this led him to nuclear physics and submarine life."

Second card: *Psychologically stable.* "It's very difficult to become a submariner—or nuke, as they call themselves— because you have to be very stable psychologically and pass all kinds of personality tests." I emphasized the correct pronunciation: sub-*mar*-i-ner, not sub-ma-*ree*-ner. "For instance, if you wanted to become a submariner but couldn't stop biting your nails, you'd probably get rejected, because it would prove you were too nervous and lacked discipline. Also, your friends and relatives get interviewed. They have to say that you're the type to stay cool under pressure."

Third card: *Education.* Gazing thoughtfully down at the hairbrush on my bureau, I rattled off all the schools my father attended. Four years at the Naval Academy in Annapolis, four months at the Officer Candidate School in Orlando, six months at the Nuclear Power Training Unit in upstate New York, and six weeks of submarine school in Groton, Connecticut. "Then my father earned his dolphins," I said, "the symbol of the submariner." I had a key chain to pass around, one I kept hidden in my socks drawer so I wouldn't ever lose it, showing two dolphins swimming toward each other, with a submarine facing you head-on between them. "This key chain is only made of nickel," I said. "The real pin is made of pure, real gold."

Fourth card: *Blue Crew, Gold Crew.* "Every submarine has two crews, the Blue and the Gold," I told the reflection of my poster of Sting. Of all the rock stars on my walls, he seemed to be listening most carefully. "My father's crew is the Blue Crew. When the Blue Crew is on the boat—and, by the way, you call a submarine a boat, not a ship—the Gold Crew is on land, getting ready to go back to sea." I talked a little about the schedule on the boat: six hours of work, six hours off, doing some training or maintenance if necessary, six hours of sleep. No days or nights, really—just shifts. Four meals a day, with the last one at midnight, if you were awake to eat it. "For recreation, sometimes my father watches a tape of a football game, commercials and all, so it feels live."

Fifth and last card: *Familygrams.* "My mother and I can send my father messages, called familygrams. But it's a little like talking to an answering machine, knowing you'll never get called back, because a submarine can't answer you back. Any outgoing signals from a sub can be picked up by enemy subs." Now I spoke to my reflection again. My eyes looked a little sad, so I tried crinkling them at the edges, but that looked even worse. So I ignored the girl with the sad eyes and finished my speech. "You're only allowed twenty words in a familygram, and even then the navy can censor as many of those words as they like. They don't want their people getting upset inside the cramped, efficient world of the submarine. You couldn't even write that your pet turtle died, if in fact you had a pet turtle and

25

if in fact it died. So, anyway, that's a little bit about Robert Gray, department head aboard a fleet ballistic missile nuclear submarine. My father likes to say that the main thing about a submarine is that there's never any room for anything, especially a mistake."

I was counting on that last line to get a laugh. I wanted this speech to be a big, splashy success, and in five weeks when my father came home I could re-create it for him. I was determined to be far more fascinating than any new baby ever could be. And it also occurred to me that if the new baby disappeared for some reason, I'd be so fascinating that my parents wouldn't grieve the loss too much. It has always amazed me—the things you tell yourself.

On the day of my speech, three kids spoke before me on the topics "Cricket—America's Next Big Sport" and "Microwaving Your Own Cosmetics" and, about a priest, "My Brother, the Father." Ms. Stapler was particularly merciless to all three of them, bellowing, "Stand up straight. Project to the back of the room. Who can hear you when you mumble? Reading from your index cards is unacceptable—you must only glance. Don't hold your arm behind your back." Ms. Stapler was over six feet tall and had stiff, tar black hair that always smelled of musty hair spray.

I wore blue jeans and a blue sweater, in honor of the Blue Crew. As Ms. Stapler clapped her hands for silence, I got up out of my chair, clutching my index cards and key chain, unexpectedly hearing Roz Spinak's words in my head: "It's scarier than you think." But I still had the Calm. I'd kept it going since my night at Aunt Beryl's nearly three weeks before, even when my mother gave me a lizard wallet for my birthday, the exact same gift as last year; even when the crib for the new Gray baby arrived; even when Aunt Beryl told me that "being a big sister is an enormous responsibility, and I ought to know"; even when, time after time, my mother lay down after work for "a twenty-minute nap" and slept through the whole night, leaving me to prepare my own dinner. The Calm had passed every test! I was so proud of it, and also it was good company.

Outside the classroom, it was cold, cold, cold. I heard the wind weaving through the branches and beating against the windows. A quick glance at the first card. *Little boy.* I launched into the part about the children's book my father loved. It was going so well I was sorry to see an empty seat in the third row—who was missing this wonderful speech? Then I realized it was my own place.

Second card. *Psychologically stable.* Right in the middle of the part about nail biting, Ms. Stapler interrupted me (Roz had warned me about that too). "Why do you suppose submariners have to stay cool under pressure?" Ms. Stapler asked.

I cleared my throat. "Because it's a stressful job," I answered.

"But why is it stressful, Ellen? You haven't told us exactly what it is your father and the rest of his crew are doing."

I was starting to feel a little shaky inside. I remembered things my father had told me a long time ago so I would understand the dark side to his work. Back then I didn't want to hear it. I preferred, "Hi, I'm Mister Proton!" But I never forgot it. "He's guarding nuclear missiles," I said. "He's making sure that the nuclear missiles are always ready to fire on their targets." I tried to take a breath but couldn't get any air into my lungs. Sixteen nuclear missiles, with 12 separate warheads, making 192 warheads in all, each one aimed at a city or town somewhere, full of people and children and dogs and parks and fountains. My father doesn't know the exact targets. Nobody on board the submarine knows that. But the missiles know exactly where they're going. Those missiles used to scare me more than any scary movie ever could.

"And if he's told to fire those missiles?" Ms. Stapler asked.

The room was very quiet. I could smell my own sweat, beneath my blue sweater. "He'll fire them," I said. "It's his job—it's what he's dedicated his whole life to."

"Continue, please," Ms. Stapler said.

Third card. *Education.* It was blurry; I could barely read it. But wait—I hadn't finished the second card yet. My head began to swirl, like litter on a windy city street. Too late, but now I understood the true nature of the Calm. It was untrustworthy, even dangerous, like the calm in the eye of a hurricane—if you moved an inch in either direction, you got swept up in it. For a moment I was afraid I'd faint. Later I wished I had, because what happened next was far worse.

"Mmm, mmmuh, mmm—" It was grotesque. I was stuttering. My mind and my mouth were pretending they didn't even know each other! I felt my neck and face flush a ghastly red. Faye Needleman and her friend Muriel Nash slapped their hands over their own mouths, smothering laughter. "Mmmuh, mmm, f-f-f-f-father . . ."

Ms. Stapler rushed over to me, her eyes wide and as green as the first leaves in spring. "That's enough, dear," she said gently, cupping my elbow in her palm, carefully leading me to my seat as if I couldn't walk properly. Who knows? Maybe I couldn't. I certainly couldn't talk. On the way, I dumped my index cards into the garbage and heard the clink of the key chain as it hit the bottom.

28

As I walked home in wind that smelled like ice, Faye Needleman and Muriel Nash caught up with me. I'd have been less surprised to see Cinderella's stepsisters.

"Hey, you did all right," Faye said, shivering in her black denim jacket. Four stud earrings dotted her left ear, and her skin, which was always very pink, was almost purple with the cold. The wind whipped her frizzy, kinky blond hair straight up. "That's one way to get out of doing a stupid speech. You broke poor old Ms. Stapler's heart. She's sure to give you a *B* at least, and I bet you only wrote half of it!"

"Yeah, right," Muriel said. "Just go duh-duh-duh, like a retard."

I couldn't believe it—they thought I stuttered on purpose! I looked hard at Muriel, waiting for her to admit this was a joke and bust out laughing. Instead she just stood there, against a ghostly, steel gray sky, pressing her legs together and shifting her weight from foot to foot. Muriel's straight brown hair was squashed beneath a black beret and hung over her right eye. Her hair always covered her right eye. Years before, this led to false rumors that she only had the left eye. Muriel was chubby all over, the way toddlers are chubby, and you could see every pound in her tight jeans and pullover.

"I used to be so proud of my father," I told them. "He once compared himself to a cop on a beat, protecting the whole world. Sure, he said, we carry nuclear weapons, but we don't ever want to use them." My stomach . . . it felt like a fist in there, tightening. "But can a cop start World War III and blow up the whole world? He's no cop! He's a monster!" I'll be thinking of you, I'd told my father just before he left. If he only knew.

"My father split when I was seven," Faye said with a

snort. "He went off with this woman who had six toes on each foot, all webbed together."

"It doesn't matter who they leave behind," I said. "They disappear anyway."

"My father's just a big blob," Muriel said, spitting a little as she spoke. "Hey, let's go, I have to pee."

Faye's lips were blue. "Muriel and I have hated our fathers for years," she said. "Ellen, join the club."

From then on, my mother started referring to Faye and Muriel as "those girls," saying things like, "Why are you always hanging around with those girls?" and "What do you see in those girls?" and "I can't understand why you chose those girls to be your friends."

I never explained it to her. I didn't choose them. They chose me. And anyway they were all right—a couple of cool customers.

I learned how to communicate with Faye and Muriel during class: a quick, disgusted look when a teacher's pet like Susie Brockleman raised her hand with the correct answer, and a snicker when she proudly delivered the wrong one; how to blot everybody else out and glance only at them, to see how they were doing. Usually their expressions told me, I'm so bored I could die!

Nearly every day, Faye and Muriel came over to my loft, or we all went over to Faye's apartment. Muriel said her place was off-limits because her father, who worked all night as a security guard, slept until three and then sat around for the rest of the afternoon in his underwear.

"If he looked like Robert Redford, I wouldn't mind," Muriel explained. "But he looks like a whale, all white and blubbery."

It was enough to keep me away from the Nash home.

30

Faye invited me to sleep over on a Saturday night in late February. I squashed a nightgown, toothbrush, and change of underpants inside a small nylon bag, and said good-bye to my mother. She was sitting heavily on the couch, as if the air itself was weighing her down.

"Mom, are you feeling all right?"

Slowly she looked up at me, her face pale and gray. "Tired," she murmured.

Her belly strained against her sky blue, tentlike maternity dress. "Tonight it looks like you're having triplets," I said. What I meant was, I didn't know pregnant women actually got so enormous, even though there was only one baby in there.

"A few more weeks, that's all," she said, closing her eyes. "Who cares if it is triplets? As long as it's over soon."

Walking the five blocks over to Faye's, I passed expensive boutiques and luxury apartments in buildings that my mother told me used to be warehouses and artists' studios. I kept feeling a nagging tug at my brain. Should I turn right around? Was my mother all right, really? I stopped a moment, and caught my reflection in the always welcoming window of my favorite store, Paper Moon. I was frowning. Take it easy, I told myself, just forget about it. She's got Faye's number. She'll call if she needs me. Behind my reflection, a bearded guy in a brown coat inside the store frowned back at me.

Faye's one-bedroom apartment always smelled of ammonia, and sometimes it was so strong my eyes stung and actually got watery. I was pretty sure this was because her cat, Pee Wee, a fat brown tabby with bad breath, sometimes peed on the faded, old gray green living room carpet. Pee Wee let you pat him on the head, and then lunged to

31

bite you. It was a lucky thing his reflexes were so slow, so you could usually pull your hand away in time.

"What's your cat's problem?" I asked Faye that night. I got there before Muriel.

"He's mean," Faye said. She was wearing a red plaid nightshirt that reached her knees. I had the feeling she'd worn it all day, and probably since the night before, even. Faye had skinny, skinny legs, though her torso and arms were thick. "He was born mean."

Pee Wee squawked and lumbered away. The lower part of his belly swayed, nearly reaching the floor. "He's got an udder, like a cow," I said. "Oh. Sorry. That was kind of rude, huh?"

Faye shrugged it off. "I guess his name doesn't fit him anymore. He used to be so little and cute. Like I used to be, see?" And she showed me a small color photo in a silver frame.

I held it under a lamp. Faye, about three years old, was wearing a red dress—and was adorable, with a big laughing smile and glowing pink skin. It must have been later that her skin got *too* pink. Two large hands were holding her tightly around her waist.

"Who's got hold of you?" I said, smiling, though the picture was making me a little sad.

"My father," Faye said, shrugging again. "My mom burned all his pictures, but this one was allowed to live 'cause it only had the hands." The picture went back to its place on the coffee table, in front of the living room couch—which was also Faye's bed. "Listen," Faye added, "don't tell Muriel, all right? She thinks it's Sylvie who's holding me."

Sylvie, Faye's older sister, lived outside San Francisco

with her boyfriend and four big dogs. Faye had been out once to see them and said the whole place smelled of dog breath.

As soon as Muriel came over, we ordered up two large pizzas with popperoni and ate them both. Then we devoured two bags of barbecue-flavored potato chips, which stained our lips rusty red. For dessert, we finished off an ancient box of vanilla fudge twirl ice cream that was more ice than it was vanilla, fudge, or twirl. I was always hungry around Faye and Muriel, and always ate until my stomach ached with the burden of digesting all that food.

"Let's clean up before your mother gets home," I said, looking around at the bent-back pizza cartons and crumpled plastic bags. I hadn't met Faye's mother yet and didn't want to make a bad impression.

"She won't be home till tomorrow afternoon," Faye said, with a growly burp. "Leave it."

Faye shoved aside the coffee table with her feet, and gruntily opened the living room couch into an already made-up, queen-size sofa bed. "Usually I just sleep on the couch, unopened," she said.

Muriel and I changed into our nightgowns, and we all curled up on the bed. I felt gritty sand between the sheets, which really gave me the creeps because this was February, a long time away from beach weather. Still, I had a pretty good time. We played the radio loud and sang along, whenever we knew the songs. That lasted until a neighbor began to bang on the wall. So then we complained about our fathers, and trashed our teachers—Faye did a not-bad imitation of Ms. Stapler's bellow: "Speaking dishonorably of your fathers is unacceptable!"

Then Faye and Muriel exchanged a significant glance.

"Ellen, it's time." Faye spoke slowly and carefully. "We're going to let you do something that nobody else has ever, ever done, besides me and Muriel."

Oh, no. Was it drugs? My whole life, my mother told me how stupid and destructive drugs were. "Your mind is taken away from you," she always said.

From behind the couch, Faye pulled out a book with a green cover and blew dust off it.

"Open it, open it!" Muriel said, giggling.

In swirly hot pink writing on the first page, I read the underlined words: *The Craig Book*. "Who is Craig?" I asked.

"Oh, my God!" Muriel said, smearing her hair down over her right eye. "Don't you remember Craig Mueller? He was with us in sixth grade, until he moved away to Milwaukee. God, he was too cute to live."

I flipped through the pages. There were signed, dated entries:

September 14
Craig wore his bleached jeans today, the ones with the rip in the behind!!! He looked at me longingly!! I think he likes me!!! Muriel.

September 22
It was so hot today and Craig was sweating. He smiled at me and said it was too hot to think. Too hot to think. He's got such an interesting mind. Faye.

But later entries were all about somebody named Mark:

May 4
*Mark has the greenest eyes!!! He's beautiful!!!!
I think he likes me!! Muriel.*

May 4
*His eyes are not repeat NOT green they are
hazel. And I don't think he likes me, I KNOW he
likes me. Faye.*

"Who is Mark?" I said. "What happened to Craig?"

"We told you before," Muriel whined at me. "Craig
moved away to Milwaukee. So then we liked Mark
Schmirren."

"But it's *The Craig Book*," I said helplessly. Was this
really less stupid than drugs?

Faye snorted. "We can't keep on buying new books, can
we? Especially when there's so many pages left in this one?
Mark started going out with Susie Brockleman, God only
knows why, so now we like Jose Romero."

"So cute," Muriel said. "He looks like that guy on TV."
Faye nodded vigorously.

Sure enough, the latest entries:

February 5
*They say Latin lovers play it cool but really
they are HOT. I want to see if Jose lives up to
the reputation. Faye.*

February 17
*Jose winked at me!! He got so embarrassed he
said he had a piece of dust in his eye! Dust in
February!!! Sure!!!! Muriel.*

"Now *you* write something," Faye said.

"Oh, no, no, no," I insisted. "This is way too personal. This belongs to you and Muriel."

"But we want you to," Muriel said. "We discussed it before, me and Faye. Besides, now that you know about it, you have to."

"Of course you don't have to," Faye said, shaking her head at Muriel's logic. "But you think Jose Romero is cute, don't you?" She bit her lip. What was she scared of?

"Jose Romero is very cute," I agreed.

"Write that!" Muriel said, pointing a chubby, pizza-smeared finger at the book.

Faye handed me a hot-pink felt-tip marker. I stared down at the page a moment, and then wrote:

February 21
Jose Romero is very cute, but I think it's gone
to his head, because he's not too friendly. Ellen.

"No, no, no," Muriel said. "You're supposed to like him! He's supposed to like you! Sometimes Faye and I fight over who he likes better. . . ."

"Never mind," Faye said. "Ellen's just a beginner. She'll catch on later." That remark sent a chill through me. Faye picked up the phone and said, "Now for the fun part. Ellen gets to call him."

"Call him? Call *who*?"

"Jose Romero. Who else are we talking about?"

Well, I put up a tremendous struggle, but somehow the phone ended up in my hand, and Jose's number got dialed, and I was the one asking a woman with a Spanish accent on the other end if Jose was home this evening. Faye's and Muriel's heads were pressed so close to the receiver I could feel their damp skin and their warm, openmouthed breathing that smelled like barbecued pepperoni.

"Yeah," Jose said, in a not too friendly way. It didn't surprise me one bit. "Who is this?"

"Ellen Cray," I said, immediately wishing I'd given Faye's name, or Muriel's. It would serve them right!

"*Who?*" Jose barked into the phone.

Faye whispered, "He's pretending he doesn't know you. Just keep on talking."

"So, how's everything going?" I said, beyond embarrassment. "What are you up to on this lovely Saturday night in February?"

"I don't know you," Jose said. He made it sound like an ancient curse. Then he hung up.

Faye and Muriel dissolved in laughter, rolling all over the bed. Pretty soon I was laughing and rolling too. The call to Jose made us giddy. Faye thrust her arm over me to drop the phone down on the floor. "Wait," I said. "Is the hook off the phone? I mean, is the phone off the hook?"

"Ellen, you make no sense at all!" Faye laughed. She snapped on the radio again, extra loud this time, and we sang extra loud, until the banger next door went back to banging.

What happened next, though I never knew what triggered it, was a nasty fight between Faye and Muriel. Suddenly Faye was red-hot boiling mad that yesterday, when Muriel gave Faye back her green shirt, there was a rip in it. I myself thought that shirt was fairly hideous, with its puffy sleeves and tight midriff, but Faye's rage had her nearly in tears. Muriel swore innocence. "Stick a needle in my eye!" she pleaded more and more desperately. "The rip was there before!" Twice Muriel grabbed my wrist—it was important to her that I believed this too. Eventually I broke

37

up the fight by getting Muriel to promise to sew the shirt, and Faye had to at least say that she believed the rip wasn't Muriel's fault.

This was hard work and left me utterly worn out. But when I told Faye and Muriel that I wanted to get some sleep, Muriel said, "No! We want to stay up all night!"

"Go right ahead," I said. "I can sleep even if you two are up and talking."

"No," Muriel said again. "It has to be everybody."

"But what if I wasn't here?" I asked her.

"Then we'd stay up, of course," Muriel replied. "But that's different."

"Never mind," Faye muttered before I could figure out the logic here. "We'll all go to sleep."

I said, "I really don't mind—"

"Three across, all right?" This time Faye cut me off. "Ellen, you're in the middle."

I lay there for a while, listening to Muriel's light snore, my eyes burning slightly. So why couldn't Faye and Muriel stay up without me? They seemed to need me now, after years of needing only each other. As an audience, as a confidante, and even, it seemed, as a referee. But I wasn't at all sure we were friends yet, real true-blue best friends. *Ellen, you're in the middle.*

Just before dawn, we woke up to the sound of yelling.

"What a mess! You little brat! Who told you your filthy friends could come over here and make such a mess!" Harsh lights went on. Mrs. Needleman stood near our feet, in the glare. She had deep lines in her face and rusty brown hair and wore a purple sweater and leather miniskirt, exposing skinny, skinny legs. "It's a school night!" she shrieked.

"Tomorrow is Sunday, Mother dear." Faye spoke with

exaggerated sweetness. But I knew she was embarrassed to the core.

"Don't get smart with me," her mother said.

My mother, who didn't like Faye and Muriel, was always friendly to them. Mrs. Needleman snorted, and then walked off, slamming the door to her bedroom.

"My mom's pissed 'cause she had to come home so early," Faye explained. "She likes to party all night."

"Who doesn't?" Muriel said.

Faye snorted too.

We all fell asleep again, and I didn't wake up until Pee Wee, his head inches away from mine, breathed his smelly fishy breath on me. Light streamed into the room. I nudged Faye and Muriel awake. We got up and put clothes on, or at least Muriel and I did. Muriel applied gobs of makeup, as usual, and I watched her carefully draw a thick line of eyeliner below her right eye, the eye that was never visible. I'd always wondered whether she did that. And then we cleaned up the place.

In daylight, Mrs. Needleman was actually much nicer. She wished everybody a groggy "good morning," and cooked up some pancakes, which tasted pretty good. We also had toast and bacon and orange juice. Pressing a wet washcloth to her forehead and describing her headache as one that could split rocks, she said to Faye, "Look, you did it again. You knocked the phone off the hook."

"What?" I said, suddenly on edge.

Mrs. Needleman went on talking. "I know what girls your age do with phones. I was your age once, impossible as that is to believe. What I can't understand is, if you knock the phone off the hook, how come you don't hear that high-pitched *beep-beep-beep* sound and then put it back properly?"

"Maybe the radio was on too loud," Faye said. "That happens sometimes."

"Well, that's just great! I'm sure to hear it later from Mr. Swencionis! Did he pound his broom against the wall again?" Faye nodded, and her mother let out a loud laugh. It was the exact opposite reaction I expected. "Oh, well," Mrs. Needleman went on, "not too many people try to call up in the dead of night."

"I've got to go," I said suddenly. "What time is it?"

"Two o'clock," Faye answered.

"Wow, so late!" I said. I got up and squashed my nightgown and underpants back inside my bag. "Thanks for the delicious breakfast, Mrs. Needleman."

"Ha, ha." Faye was laughing. "It's really only noon, Ellen. Now you can stay two more hours."

But I was out of there in two minutes.

Early Sunday afternoon, back in the loft. Silvery yellow light poured in through both big windows of the living room. The smell of apple turnovers from the bakery downstairs filled the air, and a mounted policeman clattered by on the cobblestone street—but there was Aunt Beryl, sleeping on the couch, in brown slacks, a peach sweater, and brown wool socks bunched up around her ankles.

What was going on here? I allowed the front door to slam shut.

"Ellen!" Aunt Beryl cried out, sitting up stiffly, her hair all flat on one side of head. "I tried staying up for you, but how could I? I only had a few hours' sleep last night."

"Where's my mother?" I said, as if Aunt Beryl had done something to her.

40

Aunt Beryl was clutching at her own hands. "Loretta had her baby," she said.

I blinked at her, trying to make this image and these words make some kind of sense. "Where's my mother?" I repeated.

"That's what I'm telling you." Aunt Beryl pulled at the thin skin around her knuckles. "Loretta's in the hospital. She had her baby just a few hours ago."

"You're wrong. That new baby isn't due for three more weeks. You think I'd sleep over at my friend's house if my mother was having a baby?"

"But that's just it, Ellen, nobody knew. She tried to call you"—my stomach clenched up at that—"and then had to call an ambulance. Later on, she asked a nurse to call me, to see if I could drive over here and look after you. Because you're all alone without Robert." She smiled stiffly. "Aren't you at all curious about whether it's a girl or boy?"

I peered behind the couch. "This is a big joke, right? My mother's here—she's not in any hospital. Come on out, Mom, it's all over! Aunt Beryl isn't a very good actress!" But after bolting into every room, I saw that my mother really wasn't home.

"I'm supposed to make you breakfast," Aunt Beryl said, looking quite pale. She'd never had any children, and didn't understand my demented behavior.

"I already ate breakfast. Pancakes, toast, bacon, orange juice."

"Lunch, then, later," Aunt Beryl breathed out, relieved that feeding time for the Beast was postponed. "You may visit Loretta tomorrow. She must sleep today. She had an awfully long and difficult labor. I imagine the whole experience was rather frightening, what with finding out at the hospital that her doctor'd had a stroke—"

41

"What? What are you talking about?" My heart was beating against my chest.

"Lordy," Aunt Beryl said. "Loretta especially instructed the nurse to tell me not to upset you. And now I've gone and done it. The long and difficult labor, and Dr. Walker's stroke just popped out of me."

My mother had been going to see Dr. Walker for seven years. She adored him. She went in once and she hadn't seen him for six months, and he told her he was glad she'd stopped biting her nails. "Now there's a sweet and observant doctor," she told me.

I asked Aunt Beryl, "You mean, Dr. Walker had a stroke because my mother was having a baby?"

"Don't be silly! That was Dr. Walker's job, delivering babies. His stroke occurred several days ago. He can't speak, poor man, or move his entire right side. And only fifty-seven years old. A new colleague of his filled in for him at the last moment."

I couldn't shake the image: a doctor starting to deliver my mother's baby, and then keeling over at the mere sight of it! The way Medusa turned men into stone! My brain flipped over like a pancake. "Is my mother all right?" I said. "Is she feeling all right?"

"Loretta's fine. You will be seeing her yourself after school tomorrow, as I already told you."

I had to ask Aunt Beryl all the details all over again. I'd heard every word she said, but most of them just hadn't stayed inside my head.

"You astound me, Ellen. You still haven't asked me whether it's a girl or a boy."

It wasn't so astounding. Once I found out, there wouldn't be an "it" anymore, there would be my little sister or my little brother.

"It's a boy," Aunt Beryl said, with pride. Some women are like that. A boy is an extraspectacular big deal.

"So, it's a boy," I said, trying this on as if it were a hideous green shirt with a rip in it.

"Your grandmother Anne was so thrilled! I called her very early this morning. She was a tad annoyed about that, but then she was so thrilled, saying she'd been secretly hoping for a boy all along!"

"What did Grandfather Mitchell say?"

"Nothing at all, really." In a kind of bored singsong, she quoted him: "It doesn't matter, boy or girl, as long as both mother and child are healthy." Aunt Beryl rubbed her knuckles. "He was very concerned about the long and difficult labor, and especially the last-minute doctor substitution, but I told him, get into the spirit of it! It's dramatic, like a Hollywood movie! All we needed last night was a blizzard!"

Mostly to take a break from Aunt Beryl, I took a long, long, long bath in my parents' bathroom (my bathroom doesn't have a tub). Aunt Beryl had been full of advice that afternoon. I should avoid wearing big sweatshirts and sneakers, she said, because it wasn't feminine. I must learn how to sew pretty clothes, and she could teach me. My reaching for a few chocolate chip cookies brought on a kindly reminder about weight, skin, and mood swings caused by sugar. Scientists have yet to study the mood swings caused by Aunt Beryl herself.

I was still in the tub, my body slowly turning into the Prune Creature from Outer Space, when the phone rang.

"Ellen! It's Loretta!"

Grabbing the nearest towel, I rushed naked and dripping into my parents' bedroom and spread out the towel to sit on it. Too late I realized that I'd only grabbed a face towel. "Aunt Beryl, please hang up," I said into the phone, and she did.

"Hi, sweetheart," my mother said, sounding even more exhausted than she had the day before.

"What'd you go and have a baby for? Why couldn't you wait till I got home?" I was trying to sound jokey, but I could hear that it came out sounding a little mean. The new crib stood way across the room—near the wall closest to my bedroom. Would I be hearing crying and howling all night?

"I'm sorry, El." Her voice was slow and thick. "Bad timing. That number where you were, busy, busy, busy, all night. Robert will be so upset too that he wasn't here." My father! Away on his stupid boat. "Are you getting along with Aunt Beryl?" my mother asked.

"She talks and I'm trying not to listen, if that's what you mean."

That got a little laugh out of her. "He's adorable, El," she went on. "I only saw him once, before the nurse took him away."

"Took him away? Where?"

"I'm not sure." She was falling asleep on me. "Isn't it sad, El, about Dr. Walker?"

Maybe some nurse had given her a postbaby drug or something. Already she was forgetting I wasn't even supposed to know about Dr. Walker. Besides, why would a baby get taken away? "Very sad," I agreed. "I'll see you tomorrow. You go to sleep, now."

"His name is Barry," she said. "You have a brother and his name is Barry."

Barry. Barry, Barry, Barry. That sure was a nothing name. I knew she got the *B* part from her own father's name, Burgess. My mother is Jewish, and though my father

44

is Protestant, he agreed to use names that began with *E* or *B*, after her parents. I was named after my mother's mother, Eleanor. The name Barry fit perfectly, as if a jigsaw puzzle of the Gray family was missing a crucial piece all these many years.

The next morning, Aunt Beryl asked me to please sit on a large, absorbent towel next time I ran out of the tub to talk on the phone—she tossed and turned on a soaking-wet mattress all night.

I used my father's toothbrush because I'd left mine at Faye's apartment. I planned to keep on leaving it there. Mrs. Needleman wasn't such a bad person. Maybe I could spend more time in the Needleman home.

At school, I didn't feel like mentioning the new baby boy to Faye and Muriel yet. Instead of telling them I was taking a bus uptown to the hospital after school, I said I had to visit my grandparents in the residential home.

"Bummer," Faye said. "Old people are so boring."

"My grandfather is totally senile," Muriel said, staring off at something. "He keeps calling me Brenda. That's his daughter and she died before I was even born." When I followed her gaze, it led only to a fire-prevention poster.

I'm not too crazy about hospitals, but I'd always heard maternity wards were the most cheerful places in them. A couple of nurses looked happy enough and grinned at me, but it was still a hospital and I knew most people in this building weren't feeling so hot.

My mother lay in the far corner of a rectangular beige room with one other bed occupied by a sleeping woman. A white sheet went all the way up to my mother's chin. I braced myself for my first sight of Barry, but there was no

Barry. Come to think of it, there were no babies in this room.

"Ellen," my mother said, no strength at all in her voice. From beneath the sheet, a hand slowly reached up to hold mine. "I'm so happy to see you, sweetheart."

"Where's the baby?" I said.

"Not here," she said softly. "He wasn't eating, so a nurse took him away to another ward in the hospital." Then she said something I didn't quite understand.

"What?" I said. "Hook him up to *ivy*?"

She smiled. "Hook him up to an IV. It means Barry's being fed intravenously, through a needle in his arm." I shuddered at that, but she kept on holding my hand, and her hand felt warm. "He's so tiny, El," she went on. "He's got a big head, but he's so tiny." Then she squeezed my hand hard, too hard for somebody who looked so weak, and said, "There's something wrong with him."

I pulled my hand away. "What?" I said. My stomach felt like dark, thick clouds gathering before a storm.

"It's not right, a baby that doesn't eat. This morning, I held Barry to my breast, and he didn't do anything. A nurse tapped his foot. That's supposed to stimulate sucking and swallowing. But it didn't. Even after I forced a little milk down his throat, he coughed it right back up. And he doesn't cry, El, he never cries."

"So what? That's great! Whoever heard of anybody complaining because a baby *doesn't* cry?" My whole body was tensing up.

"Last night, he didn't wake up to eat, though he must have been very hungry. It's not right, El, not to suck and swallow and cry and wake up, all those baby things."

I walked around her bed, and tried to keep my voice low

and steady. "Did the doctors tell you there was anything wrong with him?"

"No. They all said he was perfect."

"Then that's that!" I said, a little too loud. The woman in the other bed stirred and rolled over. "That's that," I repeated in a whisper. "The doctors ought to know. They're the doctors!"

"There's something else." Her voice was flat, almost mechanical. "I've seen Barry's eyes flick to the left, then to the right, very, very fast, just for a few seconds."

That didn't sound so terrible. Why was she making it sound terrible? I kept my voice even. "What did the doctors have to say about that?"

"That I probably wasn't seeing what I thought I was seeing. That I must have read something in a book that frightened me. That even if I did see it, it was nothing to worry about."

"All right, then! So there's nothing to worry about!"

My mother tightened her lips. She once told me she'd been a very rebellious teenager, but I could never picture it. Now for the first time I could see it, her defiance, as if it were a big beauty mark I never noticed before. "I know what I saw, Ellen. I held my baby in my arms. I know there's something wrong with him."

I kept walking around her bed like a tiger about to turn to butter. Why was she saying these things—to get back at me for leaving the phone off the hook? It wasn't like my mother to make up crazy stories to punish me. Punishment wasn't exactly her style, anyway. But maybe she was different now.

"Sleepy," my mother said, and fell asleep almost instantly.

"Spicy Swedish meatballs over broad egg noodles," was what Aunt Beryl called dinner. I pushed aside the meatballs because they hurt my stomach. Aunt Beryl, frantically up-beat, talked on and on about her own visit to my mother earlier that day: "Didn't Loretta look lovely! Wretched and exhausted, of course, but lovely. Too bad we couldn't see little Barry. But we'll see him very soon! Won't that be fun, a little bouncing baby boy? Ellen, dear, don't just eat the noodles. You need the protein."

I stayed away from the hospital on Tuesday, and instead played records over at Faye's apartment. She showed me Muriel's repair job on the green shirt—a zigzag of yellow thread!

Wednesday morning the air smelled of snow. Aunt Beryl said she couldn't possibly neglect her consulting business for one hour longer, and left just before I went to school. And that afternoon my mother and her new baby boy came home.

PART TWO

The Lump

4

Light snow fell and stuck. And I was getting my first look at Barry. I'd never thought babies were heartbreakingly adorable, and Barry was no exception. Tiny, beige, wrinkled, and limp, with a large, bald, bluish head. So this is my little brother, I thought. Nothing here to get too worked up about. But that didn't stop Loretta from insisting every hour on the hour that there was something wrong with him.

She was Loretta to me now. She was Barry's mother.

"The child is absolutely fine," I told her that night at dinner.

"Oh, really?" Loretta said. "You can see how it is."

It was true that she could only feed him with a bottle, and that she had to use a nipple with an extra large hole in it, and that he didn't suck, so she had to tilt his head way back to let the formula trickle down his throat. And that was just the start of it. Feedings took up to two hours. And all through every one of them, Barry gulped loudly, and let out long gurgles that sounded like guys who clear their throats so they can spit on the curb. Also, Barry splattered milky white liquid all over himself.

"Look how he sleeps," Loretta said one morning, gripping my shoulders as we stood over Barry's crib. "He's sleeping on top of his arms. You'd think he'd wriggle around, wouldn't you, and pull his arms out from under his tummy? But two hours ago he was in this exact same position. It's like he doesn't know he has arms."

"Mom, he can't know much, at less than a week old." I squirmed beneath her grasp. "Besides, maybe you're watching him too closely. Anything looks weird from too close up. If you magnify strands of hair two hundred times, you think you're looking at a forest full of monster trees."

But Loretta wouldn't let go of me. "I have to wake him up for every single feeding, for every single diaper change. He still doesn't cry. If I show him a bright, shiny object, he doesn't look at it. He still does that flicking thing with his eyes, back and forth."

"Where's Barry going to sleep when he outgrows this crib?" I asked, trying to more or less change the subject.

Loretta sighed, as if Barry's outgrowing a crib was a wonderful event that might never happen. "I don't know," she said. "Maybe we'll put up a couple of walls in the living room and create a whole new room."

"No way!" I burst out. "The loft should stay perfect!"

Loretta finally let go, shrugging me away, and went on with her new career in life—endlessly watching Barry, a troubled look in her eyes.

I've always liked Soho, even though it's become one of New York's richest neighborhoods and we haven't gotten rich along with it. But in the first days of Barry's life, I began to ache for Connecticut, the same way Dorothy longed for black-and-white Kansas even in exciting, color-soaked Oz. In Connecticut, we used to live in Groton. Not the greatest name for a town. It sounded like an old, damp, smelly dungeon. But only a few miles away there was Mystic—a name that sounded like clouds of swirling colors with shapes inside you can't quite make out.

When I was five, my favorite place was the aquarium at Mystic. One day, I begged my mother to sit through four marine mammal shows there, because I adored watching Mindy, the sea lion who refused to do tricks. The other sea lions climbed up on a tilted platform and barked and waved a front flipper around. Mindy simply tossed her head back and looked away—what spirit! At the end of the fourth show, the trainer apologized to the whole audience, telling us that he and Mindy had had a fight that morning, and Mindy was still mad at him. I loved her even more for it.

I even missed the sad parts of Connecticut. Once, my mother took me to watch a battleship come in so I could see the balloons and laugh at the clowns and hear the loud brass band. But when Daddy didn't get off the ship with all the other sailors, I cried. "Daddy's on a submarine," she told me, wiping away my tears with a white handkerchief embroidered with tiny purple flowers. "Daddy has to dock his submarine in Scotland. Then Daddy flies to New York and takes a bus home." I could never explain it to her—that Daddy was always piling sadnesses on me, one on top of the other.

The following weekend Loretta took Barry to some new doctors, but after each appointment came home furious and disgusted. "Why won't they admit they're seeing what's right in front of their eyes?" she said, her thin arms clasped around Barry. "But instead of looking, they just talk. They say that every child has his own unique speed of development. Or they say that boys develop more slowly than girls. Or they say Barry's lucky to have such a devoted mother. It's as if I hit a button and get the recording!"

"Mom, has it ever occurred to you that these doctors might possibly be right?"

Loretta tightened her lips. "No," she said. "Not for an instant."

Barry was eleven days old by the time Robert came home from patrol. I never saw him so excited, kissing me so quickly it felt like an insect landing. Then he rushed over to Barry in his crib.

"He's beautiful," Robert said, his icy blue eyes dancing and glistening.

Loretta started in right away: "But look at him carefully, Robert. See how he's barely moving? Feel his leg, how tight it is? Watch his eyes."

"He's beautiful, Loretta," Robert repeated.

"You're as bad as the doctors!" she cried. "I wish you'd been around more when Ellen was a baby. Then maybe you'd know how babies are supposed to behave!"

And so began our month together.

That night we had our first dinner as "a family of four," as Loretta began calling us, at a brand-new Italian restaurant around the corner. It was cozy and small, with a low ceiling, soft lights, pale pink roses in tiny Perrier bottles, and a single-page menu written in Italian.

"Where does it say spaghetti with meatballs?" I asked.

Robert, who had put on a blue jacket and a tie with his dolphin insignia all over it, pointed to penne Bolognese. "That's meat sauce," he explained, "the closest thing."

"It's twenty dollars!" I said. "It used to be four dollars at the coffee shop across the street!" I glanced at Barry and felt a pang for the old coffee shop, now a vacant lot.

"This evening is an occasion," Loretta said. She was wearing a pretty black wool dress and had a black-and-white scarf draped glamorously over her shoulders. So what if spaghetti costs twenty dollars?" She was adjusting Barry, who wore a bib and blue jumpsuit. He was putting up zero resistance. Wherever Loretta placed an arm or a leg, that was exactly where it stayed.

"How's my girl?" Robert said.

He was looking right at me, so I guessed he was referring to me. "Fine," I said, and looked away. At the next table, a very handsome man with a strong jaw and intense dark eyes leaned forward eagerly, placing his hand like a turtle shell over his date's. I could almost feel that hand. She had on a turquoise silk dress. Her long, clean, yellow hair fell into the curve of her back.

"I missed you," Robert said.

I felt as if he'd woken me out of a deep sleep. "But you've always told me that the people on your boat are like one big happy family," I said. "The crew are the kids, the captain is the daddy, the executive officer is the mommy, and the other officers, including you, are the big brothers."

Robert smoothed back his brown hair. For the first time since his return, I took a good look at him. His hairline was receding. That, or his forehead was growing. His nose looked a bit raw from a cold—common enough for returning submariners, because the air on the boat is cleaner than the air we breathe every day. But it wasn't just the cold. He looked . . . pale, washed out. Like less of a person. He certainly seemed different. Or was the difference in how I was seeing him? "You're correct," he responded. "In some ways the hierarchy on a submarine is similar to that of a family. But it isn't an actual family. It isn't even a decent substitute."

He's got an answer for everything, I decided. After fourteen years in the military, he had developed one of those highly trained, disciplined minds, capable of defending any position logically. He once told me he got paid to think a certain way and not get emotional about it. I used to think my father was warm and strong and solid. But look at his mind! It was as rigid and impersonal as a traffic bump!

Robert sniffed, blew his nose. "What happened to the sweet girl I left behind?"

So, I was different for him too. The handsome man at the next table poured wine for the woman, smiling at her as if nobody else existed for him and nobody else ever would. My throat tightened.

"I understand," Robert said. "You're growing up. Sometimes it feels as if the whole world has turned upside down. I know. I remember."

But when he was a child he knew exactly what he wanted to do with his life—play with atoms all day long—and that was all he'd ever done. When did his world ever turn upside down? "You can't possibly know," I said.

"Ellen!" Loretta frowned at me. "Don't speak to your father that way. We're a family, the four of us. That's our strength." And she gave Barry a hug.

"This is to be expected," Robert said. "This is all part of it."

"Part of what?" I said. "A passing phase? You think you've located the problem, and can order it out of existence? But we're not on your boat and you're not my officer!"

"No," Robert said with emphasis. "I'm your father and you're my daughter."

There was no responding to that. I sank back in my chair.

"Ready, folks?" our waitress asked, bright and cheerful.

After giving my order, I barely said a word until the food arrived. Then I started to eat, shoveling it in, not tasting any of it. I began to get a stomachache. Robert said something about how "coming home is more complicated than a hug" and "home is never the same because the people are never the same." With conversation like this, you didn't need to eat fast to get a stomachache.

Loretta took a bottle out of her bag, tilted Barry's head way back, as usual, and calmly began to feed him.

"Mom, are you serious?" I said, appalled. Yes, she was. Here, in this tiny, glowing restaurant, where everything was beautiful, hushed, and elegant, Barry began to gulp and gurgle, thoroughly drenching his bib and blue jumpsuit with formula and thick white mucus. I shuddered and went stiff. Disappear! I commanded my body. Disappear, like fog into wind!

"That's some motor," Robert said admiringly. But he squirmed around in his chair when he said it.

Loretta kept on feeding Barry as if she were home, surrounded by the yellow walls of our own kitchen. I prayed that the handsome man at the next table wouldn't notice Barry, but he was making terrible faces at his date, and she swiveled around to stare at Barry down a long, thin nose. The handsome man caught our waitress's eye and whispered something to her. Then the waitress approached us.

"Ah, I'm sorry," she began, smiling hugely, "but I'm afraid your child is disturbing several of our diners."

"We're your diners too," Loretta said. "We're not disturbed."

"Ah, yes, but your child is actually making quite a bit of noise there, and, well—"

"Well what?" Loretta said roughly. "You're not seriously asking us to leave, are you?" There was that defiance again. Was it now a permanent part of her, as much as her prettiness and humor were?

"Ah, perhaps you could feed your child later on. . . ."

I shut my eyes. It was the next best thing to disappearing. Why did Loretta have to bring Barry here? Why did she have to stand up to a waitress who was only doing her job? Why wasn't it me at the next table, with a handsome man pressing my hand and interested in nothing but me?

I had to open my eyes because Robert had ordered tartufo and, well, there was no saying no to tartufo—ice cream and brownie covered with a chocolate shell and a cherry in the middle. The handsome man and his date skipped dessert and asked for the check. Loretta went right on feeding Barry.

As March went by, Loretta visited doctor after doctor, and Robert seemed more and more baffled by her stubbornness. They all told her what the first set of doctors had told her. "Why dispute the professionals?" he asked her. In my father's language, *professional* meant "top of the line."

My parents didn't exactly fight about it. Worse than that. Loretta retreated into a kind of private space with Barry, curling up with him in the rocking chair and murmuring to him.

Robert stayed by himself, mostly, although I think he would have liked my company. "Your mother's not being rational," he said to me one evening, as I washed the dinner dishes. "Perhaps this is a kind of postpartum reaction."

"We all have our own theories," I said briskly.

"What's yours, Ellen?"

I cleared my throat. "I'm still working on it," I said. My

58

stomach hurt. It was always hurting. I've got to get out of here, I thought, and soon.

So I began living at Faye Needleman's, eating dinner there and sleeping over almost every night, adjusting to the smell of ammonia, and the sandy sheets, and to sleeping near Faye, who thrashed around all night as if fighting off an attacker. I even started filling up pages in *The Craig Book*, writing down that Jose Romero stared at me with passionate lust and longing, when really he was giving me looks that said, *Are you that crazy girl who called me?*

Loretta was far too wrapped up in Barry to notice my absence—but Robert did. "I never get to see you," he said, when he caught a glimpse of me one afternoon. I was dropping off laundry. "You're never home anymore."

He should talk about not being home! He could write a book on the subject.

"Things are so awful at home," I told Faye and Mrs. Needleman over fried chicken TV dinners one night. We always ate at a card table in the living room, and almost always ate fried chicken TV dinners. Sometimes they came with peach cobbler, sometimes apple-cranberry crumb. "I'm practically not speaking to anybody."

"It's better that way," Mrs. Needleman said, sucking out a thread of fried chicken from between her front teeth. "Talking only leads to fighting, believe me. Ellen, if you really want to cry over something, take a look at food prices. These dinners cost an arm and a leg, and what do they put in them? Legs! It's all dark meat!"

"But I like dark meat," Faye said.

"That's not the point!" Mrs. Needleman glared at Faye.

Faye kept her clothes in a small bureau in her mother's room, and she set aside half of one drawer for me. The creepy thing was, I could swear that some of my clothes

59

were being worn—and not by me or by Faye, who I saw every day in school. One day my blue sweater smelled of beer. And once I found watermelon red lipstick on the lapel of my white blouse. I had a strange thought. Was it Mrs. Needleman who had ripped Faye's green shirt, and not poor Muriel?

On a Tuesday night in mid-March, Faye and I sat on the couch and watched an old TV movie about a beautiful woman whose brain got transplanted into the body of an okay-looking woman. Naturally she was very depressed about this. During a commercial, Mrs. Needleman said to me, "You eat quite a lot of meals here, am I right?" I nodded at her, and she went on, her voice way up high, "Perhaps at some point you could feed the cookie jar? I'm sure your parents would want you to."

"The cookie jar?" I looked at Faye. She wouldn't take her eyes off the TV, even though a panty hose commercial was on. But her jaw and forehead were throbbing. That told me she was gnashing her teeth, something Faye did sometimes. "Mrs. Needleman, do you mean I should bring cookies?"

"The cookie jar looks so empty these days," Mrs. Needleman said, jutting her chin at a large white cookie jar with a lightninglike crack in it, over on the kitchen counter.

I got up, walked over to the cookie jar, and peered inside. There was money in it, three dollar bills and a bunch of dimes. With a rush down my neck that felt like an itchy rash, I understood what was expected of me. "I . . . don't have any with me now," I said. "I've got some saved up at home. I'll bring it next time."

"That will be fine," Mrs. Needleman said.

Faye continued to stare, unblinking, at the TV. Of course she heard the whole thing. Did she think I was supposed to put money in the cookie jar too? I didn't know whether to feel sorry for Faye and Mrs. Needleman, struggling to get along in a single-parent household. I wasn't at all sure what to feel.

My savings consisted of several weeks' allowance, twenty-four dollars. On my next visit, I placed it inside the cookie jar. Neither Faye nor Mrs. Needleman said a word to me about it. Over the next couple of weeks, I put in another sixteen.

One morning, I heard Faye and Mrs. Needleman, behind the closed door of Mrs. Needleman's bedroom. The shower was on, but it didn't drown out their voices. Faye was pleading for money to buy a denim miniskirt at the Gap. "You've already got a denim miniskirt," Mrs. Needleman replied.

"But this one is so cute! It's got studs."

"Well, if you want it so very badly, tell your little friend to put in more!"

"It's her parents—they're too cheap," Faye said. "They only give her eight dollars a week, plus money for school lunches. I looked in her wallet. She's not holding out on us—not like I thought she was."

At breakfast I put on a good act, pretending I hadn't heard any of it. But after school I went slinking back home. Back to Robert and Loretta and Barry. At least there was no sand in the sheets.

And did I ever sleep! The last few days of March, I came home from school and headed straight for bed, falling into deep, lovely, dreamless sleep that lasted until morning, interrupted only by dinner and homework.

On Robert's last night, Loretta wanted all of us to go out again, but I said I had a stomachache (which I did). So then the two of them went out and I got stuck home with Barry! "Keep an eye on Barry, will you?" Loretta said. "Other babies cry to be picked up and held. Barry doesn't express it, but he needs it just as much."

I was hoping to go through life never having to touch Barry, but Loretta made such a big deal out of it. Half an hour after they left, I looked at Barry in his crib. He was groggy, eyelids bobbing up and down. I lifted him up under the arms, and held him against my chest. It was like holding a ball of warm dough. Soft. Filled with nothingness. I put him back down again. His eyelids dropped, and he fell asleep, not moving an inch. He's just a lump! I thought. My brother, the Lump. "I don't know you," I said to him, much the same way Jose Romero had said it to me.

Later that night, Loretta woke me up to watch her all-time favorite comedians, Bob and Ray, on a rerun of the "Tonight Show." She sounded more like her old, cheerful, pre-Barry self. Was she actually taking a night off?

"Is Daddy still up too?" I said.

"Yes, we'll all watch together!" I shook my head, but Loretta nodded. "Oh, come on, you must! Bob was introducing Ray. He told the audience, 'I have with me tonight the world's most modest man.' Ray interrupted him and said, 'Well, not *the* most modest.' "

It was pretty funny, but I refused to laugh. "I'm still asleep," I told her. "Asleep and dreaming."

"Honestly, Ellen," Loretta said, as she left my room, "you're taking everything so seriously these days, especially yourself."

"Look who's talking!" I told my duck lamp. "The lady who visits every doctor in the yellow pages!" I knew I was a little old for that lamp, but some attachments are hard to break.

The following morning, Loretta looked at Robert with a soft, teary, I-miss-you-already look in her eyes. Robert held her in his arms, and I couldn't help noticing what a good-looking couple they were.

When Robert said good-bye to me, he handed me something. It was an African violet, with very pretty, small purple flowers and thick green leaves. "Will you take care of this plant while I'm away?" he said. "I'd like to see it blooming when I get back."

I placed it on my windowsill, where it faced the back alley and a row of apartments on the next block. It got plenty of light, but I kept on forgetting to water it, even as I watched it turn brown, wither, and die.

5

"Mom, isn't it time you went back to work?"

We were finishing up breakfast early one Monday morning, and Loretta was wiping Barry's face with a washcloth. She was forever cleaning him. "My maternity leave ended two weeks ago," she said, still wiping away, though by now Barry's face was spotless.

I inhaled cool, fresh spring air from our open windows. "So, what's this, vacation time?" I pressed her. Loretta was a librarian at a library branch in Greenwich Village.

Barry whimpered. He did that nowadays. The Lump That Whimpered. Also, he had learned how to cry. Not much, but often enough for Loretta's most recent doctor to point out, "See? And you were so very worried because Barry never cried."

"I quit," Loretta said.

"What!" I cried out. Loretta flinched. Barry, as usual, just lay there. "You always told me how important it is to work, and how much you loved doing work that was useful! You studied so hard to get your master's! And whatever happened to having a life of your own?"

"Ellen, shhh. I'm not happy about it, but what else can I do? I'm afraid to take Barry to a day-care center or even leave him with a baby-sitter. He's not a healthy baby."

That again.

Loretta hugged Barry, who began to drool all over his clean chin. Rubbing his back lightly, kissing a faint brown fuzz ball of hair, she whispered, "That's my good boy, my sweet, sweet baby."

She likes him, I realized. What's in it for her?

In mid-April I showed up for softball tryouts in Central Park. Ms. Moore, small and tough, nipped at everybody's heels like a terrier: "I hope you're all proud of yourselves! You've all let yourselves get completely out of shape this winter! I hope you're all terribly, terribly proud!" It amazed me that adults wondered why kids were so sarcastic.

Roz Spinak was there, talking with a small group of girls. I heard her say, "So, if she dies, she dies!" Then they all cracked up. I wouldn't have minded hearing the beginning to this joke. But I was friends with Faye and Muriel, still.

I messed up a few plays. I just wasn't getting with it. "I'm disappointed in you, Ellen Gray," Ms. Moore said with a smirk, as if all my promise and potential were gone with the wind.

I left early and never went back. Later I found out that Susie Brockleman had been given my position, third base. I wanted to dial 911 and report a robbery! But Faye and Muriel said that softball was a big waste of time.

It was June when Barry began to snore. He had a whole collection of snores. So now he could be as noisy at night as he was at mealtime. He could snore like an old, old man; he could rattle like a jackhammer; and he could roar like a car with a broken muffler. Walls were no match for these snores. Several times he woke me up. Worse than that, his snores pierced my head and gave me weird, scary dreams about earthquakes and swarms of bees.

Then one morning Barry flipped over—literally, like an egg in a frying pan. Flat on his tummy one moment, and flat on his back in the next, a look of surprise in his eyes. Loretta's lips turned white. "You never did that," she said.

"I wish I could. He's a Mexican jumping bean!"

Loretta touched Barry's forehead. She was forever touching him. "He's just not in charge of what's happening," she said.

Neither am I, I wanted to say.

Barry flipped over several more times during the next few weeks, and then returned to typical Lump behavior. Loretta said he sometimes lay awake at night for hours, just looking up. "I don't sleep, either," she said. "I watch him and wonder what he's thinking about."

Sometimes I felt sorry for her.

Seventh grade ended with a special assembly, where Ms. Stapler got up on stage and made a speech of her own, about how we had reached the end of the beginning of junior high school. That phrase stuck in my head—the end of the beginning. But what was ending, and what was beginning? All I knew was, it had nothing to do with junior high.

Robert came home for July, and the two of us got to watch Barry staying pretty much the same and Loretta getting a lot worse. She bought a Snugli for Barry—a kind of pouch for a baby, like a backpack you wear in the front— and started taking walks with him and Robert at three in the morning. Why? "Barry sleeps much better afterward," she explained, dark circles beneath her eyes.

In August I had to watch all this by myself. I wasn't doing much of anything else, anyway. Loretta used to brush her hair until it fell, shimmering, to her shoulders, now she tied it back with a rubber band. One morning she started to wash her hair with the rubber band still in it! "I'm too tired," she murmured, as I cut the rubber band out from tangled clumps of wet hair. "I can't go on like this much longer."

That same afternoon, a lovely, warm Tuesday, Faye wanted the three of us to see a movie I knew was going to be terrible. I voted no. Muriel, the tiebreaker, not surprisingly voted for Faye's movie. So we went, and it *was* terrible, all about kids who go to Florida during spring break for guess what—and nobody once mentioned birth control, or AIDS, or love, even.

"That was so stupid!" I said when it was over.

"You have to admit," Faye said, "the guy who told the girl he was a law student when really he'd flunked out of law school was cute."

"I liked the guy who was so shy he'd never even kissed a girl," Muriel said.

"That's what I mean!" I sighed. "The actor playing that guy was obviously good-looking, obviously very experienced with girls, obviously . . . oh, never mind."

"Want to sleep over tonight?" Faye asked me. "My mom's been asking about you lately."

Oh? I thought. You still don't have the denim miniskirt? "I've got a stomachache," I said. Which I did.

"You always have a stomachache!" Faye grumbled.

I went home and knew right away that something had happened while I was gone. Loretta was sitting on the couch with Barry asleep in her lap. I'd seen this a thousand times before, but this time Loretta was crying.

"Mom," I said. "Mom, what's the matter?" I tried to make it sound casual. I sat down in the rocking chair.

"There *is* something wrong with Barry," she said, still crying. I'd heard this at least a thousand times, but for the first time it sounded real and final. "I brought Barry to a day-care center—"

"What! But you've said for months—"

"I remember what I said, El. But I was so exhausted. I just had to go, anyway. And now I wish I'd gone a lot sooner. Things began to fall into place right away." Then the tears stopped and her words poured out in a rush. "The day-care center was full of babies. They were all sitting up and babbling and crying—all the usual baby things. There was a woman in charge, and she asked how old Barry was. Just over six months, I told her. Then she asked why he wasn't sitting up, why he wasn't even holding his head up. When I said he never did, she looked very sad suddenly, crushed, really, and said, 'We can't take care of your son. Clearly there's something wrong with him.' Well, I started to cry, and she cried too and kept saying how very sorry she was, but I said, no, no, no, you don't understand, my heart is breaking but I'm so relieved. Somebody believes me at last."

"But Mom—she's just a lady in a day-care center! How can she be right, and a doctor's wrong? *Eleven* doctors are wrong?"

Loretta smiled. "She made an appointment for me and Barry with doctor number twelve tomorrow," she said.

"This one's supposed to be a first-rate diagnostician. Ellen, we'll finally, finally learn what's wrong with Barry." She put Barry down on the couch, stood up, and said she was going to call Robert in Connecticut.

Barry began to whimper. "You'd better be all right," I warned him, shaking a finger at him.

Loretta and Barry were away for six whole hours the next day. How long a line could there be, in front of Doctor Number Twelve's office? When Loretta finally came home, I was picking at a peanut-butter-and-jelly sandwich in the kitchen. Her expression seemed quite cool and detached, like a mannequin, and she was standing very straight, holding Barry in a new way, low down on her body, with his legs around her hip, froglike.

"Where's the Snugli?" I said. What I really wanted to ask was, Where's my mother? I wasn't even sure I knew the woman in front of me. Had pod people taken over Doctor Number Twelve's office and sent this automaton home in her place? But Barry looked exactly the same. Why hadn't they snatched him instead?

"The Snugli is in my bag." She spoke in a slower, more measured voice. An older voice, it sounded like. "Ellen, the doctor and I talked for five hours, but the time went by like five minutes."

Loretta sat down, arranging both of Barry's legs around one of hers. This was something new too. "Barry has cerebral palsy," she said simply, as if remarking, Barry spilled milk on his chin.

"He does not! That's all wrong!" I had to make her understand. "Those kids are all weird and spastic!"

"There are many different types." I heard patience in Loretta's voice, as if she were back in the library and explaining to a difficult borrower that her branch hadn't yet received a certain book. "In fact, cerebral palsy covers so many different conditions, the doctor said it's almost a garbage-can term."

"Garbage is right!"

"Barry has the ataxic kind, El. It means he'll always have poor balance and depth perception, and trouble walking, and trouble speaking, and he may have mental retardation—"

"What? Now you're telling me he's a retard?" It was one of Muriel's favorite words—retard. "So, all right, what's the big deal, how do you cure it?"

Loretta blinked at me. "There's no cure," she said. "This is permanent brain damage. The connection between Barry's brain and Barry's muscles has been permanently damaged—"

"Stop it," I said. I wished I could put my hands over my ears and hum. "This is garbage. You're forgetting eleven whole doctors. This just makes the score eleven to one!"

"Most people in my situation see an average of fourteen doctors before getting an accurate diagnosis. It's even got a name—doctor shopping." She took an envelope out of her bag, and poured out some white pills. "The eye flicking, Ellen. Those were tiny seizures. Every night and every morning, Barry's got to take this antiseizure medication, phenobarbital. The doctor warned me it could knock Barry out, or make him spacey."

"But he's always that way!"

"No, he's not. He can be quite active sometimes, if you redefine what you think 'active' means. The doctor explained everything. Barry can't swallow properly. That's why eating is so difficult, and why he snores. Barry's muscles sometimes tighten up at night. That's why Barry sometimes can't sleep. The flipping over was classic for kids with cerebral palsy. I wish I'd known that! I got so scared—and it was normal. Normal for our Barry."

Barry was looking at me. For the first time I noticed that his eyes were blue. Before that, I guess I'd only thought of them as eyes, not much color at all, like clear marbles.

"Tomorrow I'm taking Barry over to United Cerebral Palsy, on Twenty-third Street. They've got something called an Infant Stimulation Program." She rooted around in her bag. "The doctor also gave me this." It was an orange book: *Handling the Young Cerebral Palsied Child at Home*, by Nancie R. Finnie. "Babies learn about the world through their senses." Loretta was actually getting excited about this. I tried not to listen. I couldn't help listening. "Babies like to crawl over to things, and pick them up, and put them in their mouths, and then watch them fall. Barry won't be able to do all that, so we'll have to fill in the gaps for him. We'll have to show him how far away something is, because he won't be able to tell just by looking. We'll have to show him that a nearby object is within reach. Strange as it sounds, we'll have to become active little babies for him."

"No, I won't become a retard, just like him!" My stomach felt like long, thin knives were slicing through it.

Loretta looked at me long and hard, and then said, "I didn't cry when I heard Barry had CP"—she was using the lingo already—"even though my heart felt wrapped in ice. I didn't cry when I heard Barry would never walk or talk properly, and might not think right, either. But Ellen . . ." She paused. Her eyes were clear and direct. "You mustn't ever treat Barry like a freak."

There was only one thought anywhere in my brain. So my prayer had been answered. But something had gone

71

horribly wrong. In Aunt Beryl's sewing room I'd asked God to make the baby disappear. Now God was punishing us both.

I hadn't killed Barry—I only wrecked him.

Loretta worked with Barry all day at UCP, and loved it. "The kids are adorable—the teachers are fantastic!" she gushed. She'd found a new place in life. Where could I go?

Robert visited for a few days just before his next patrol. When he first saw me, he gave me a big hug. "I guess my theory was wrong, honey," he said. Then he spent most of his time with Loretta, poring over the orange book together, whispering late into the night, while I lay doubled up on my bed. Sometimes, when the city was absolutely quiet, I heard a train whistle from a real train. It had to be over in New Jersey, somewhere, because Manhattan doesn't have diesel trains. It sounded so lost and beautiful, like a sweet voice calling out in fog. It made me cry. I'd never cried over a sound before.

During Robert's visit, Loretta asked me to cook spaghetti for dinner one night. As I watched the spaghetti boil and bounce, I had a sudden and very eerie feeling. My future. It was gone. I mean, I felt I had no future. I dumped the spaghetti into the sink and stared down at it. I couldn't believe it. I'd forgotten to put a colander down. I had to start all over again.

Robert left, and Aunt Beryl called to arrange a visit during the Labor Day weekend. She invited herself, as usual, but Loretta told me, "It's just as well. I want to explain about Barry in person, not over the telephone."

Aunt Beryl arrived carrying her overnight bag and wearing an orange leisure suit with almost-but-not-quite matching orange lipstick. She gave Barry a big orange kiss just below his mouth. "How's my Barry?" she said, dropping down beside him and Loretta on the couch. "Oh, Loretta, he's the best-behaved boy in the whole world! Anne's been singing his praises too. She says he's exceptionally well mannered, for a baby."

Loretta half smiled at me over in the rocking chair. Earlier that day she'd told me, "Lots of parents say their handicapped children are the most lovable, because they're too docile to make any trouble."

Before Loretta could say a word, Aunt Beryl announced she was taking a class in aerobic dancing. "You should see the instructor. *Skinny.*" Aunt Beryl held up her pinky. "She hops around like an anorexic kangaroo"—the pinky bobbed up and down—"while the rest of us are having conniption fits!" Then she lengthily described a dance routine I couldn't picture.

"You're certainly looking very trim," Loretta said politely. "Aerobic dancing is very good for you."

"Why, thank you, Loretta!" Aunt Beryl glowed. She doesn't get too many compliments, I realized.

"Beryl, there's something I have to tell you. It's about Barry."

Aunt Beryl stretched her neck up, preparing herself.

Loretta plunged right into it. "He's got cerebral palsy," she said.

Aunt Beryl's eyelids fluttered. After a brief silence, she asked Loretta a handful of very carefully phrased questions, about how Loretta "learned this bit of news," and what were "the consequences." After each one of Loretta's answers, Aunt Beryl licked her lips and remarked, "I see, I see." But then she asked a couple of the same questions over again.

"I'll make some tea," I announced, and made an escape into the kitchen, closing the door behind me. I could still hear the tones of their voices but not the actual words. The kettle whistled.

When I got back to the living room, Aunt Beryl had managed to slide completely away from Barry, until her back was up against the opposite arm of the couch. From there, she was eyeing Barry as if he were a new, impossible aerobic-dance routine. "I'm not sure I understand how this happened, Loretta," Aunt Beryl said.

"There's nothing to understand," Loretta said wearily. "It happened. Apparently these things can just happen."

Aunt Beryl accepted a cup of tea from me, her little finger flicking up. "Thank you, Ellen. Nearly boiling, just the way I prefer it. I can't drink it the way Loretta likes it—lukewarm. Loretta, did you take any harmful medicine while you were pregnant? Did you take a spill somewhere? Maybe you tripped and landed on your stomach, when you were getting out of the subway."

"I didn't fall," Loretta said, blowing and blowing on her tea. "I didn't take any medicine, only prenatal vitamins."

"Maybe you were much too old to bear a child safely. Were you and Robert arguing? Were you worried about him while he was on the submarine? Didn't a Soviet submarine go down while you were pregnant? Nothing like this has ever been in our family. Is it in Robert's?"

Loretta deflected every little suggestion, but each one seemed to pierce her a tiny bit. Suddenly Aunt Beryl put her hand to her cheek. "You mustn't tell Anne!" she cried. "This news would kill her!" I wasn't all that surprised when Loretta agreed, at least to putting it off for a while. If Aunt Beryl asked this many questions, how many would Grandmother Anne think of?

Aunt Beryl came a little too close to the wrong sort of question when she asked Loretta, "What's the matter with Ellen? She's awfully quiet for such a little chatterbox."

"Ellen is fine," I said quickly. "Ellen's never been better."

Aunt Beryl went to bed very early, and packed up the first thing in the morning. Just before leaving, she leaned toward Barry but didn't kiss him. "Perhaps I shouldn't," she said. "I caught a chill last night."

I didn't know why that bothered me. I hadn't ever kissed Barry myself.

Eighth grade was almost exactly like seventh, except that now there were new seventh-graders in the halls, looking terrified and barely old enough to cross the street alone. Not that I had reason to feel high-and-mighty. Sometimes when I looked down at my hands, they were shaking.

I hadn't killed Barry. I only wrecked him.

In English, we were assigned two books I really wanted to read ever since hearing about the Brontë sisters—*Jane Eyre* and *Wuthering Heights*. But by the time I reached the end of a paragraph, I'd forgotten the beginning of it. So my book reports were entirely based on Cliffs Notes, and when I handed them in, I barely recognized my own handwriting—it looked like an old person's.

Math made absolutely no sense. Let $x = 12$. What was that supposed to mean? I did all right on my math tests because diagonally in front of me sat Ray Frost, math whiz. I didn't think of it as cheating, not really. I considered it a modern, time-saving convenience, like a dishwasher.

Lucky me, I had Ms. Stapler again, this time for communications. She'd given me a B on my speech, as Faye predicted, but ever since had looked at me like I was a left-alone puppy tied up to a parking meter. I flunked two out of three pop quizzes—no geniuses were sitting within my field of vision—and Ms. Stapler scribbled "See me after class" across the top of the second one, in loopy red writing. So I saw her after class. She took my hand, and her hand felt like cool glass. "Ellen," she said gently, "I know you're a bright girl. But you're failing communications and so far the material isn't very difficult. What will happen later on, when the material increases in difficulty?"

I wanted to pull my hand away, back off from the smell of musty hair spray. "Ms. Stapler, my parents are getting divorced," I said.

Her light green eyes widened. "Oh, you poor dear! I'm so very sorry to hear that. I know all too well what you're going through. Let's not worry about those *F*s, all right? Here's a late pass for your next class."

I had just discovered another modern, time-saving convenience.

One Saturday afternoon the bell rang downstairs. Loretta was out grocery shopping.

"Hi!" Faye's voice came up the intercom. "Muriel and I were just hanging out doing nothing and figured you were too."

So true. I buzzed them in.

"Are you alone?" Muriel said, as she came inside.

"Well . . . it's just me and Barry."

"Oh, just you and the party animal, huh?" Faye said with a laugh.

Right then, I decided to tell them about Barry. After all, we were supposed to be friends. And, anyway, Aunt Beryl knew. They should know too.

"You've heard of cerebral palsy?" I asked them.

"Sure," Muriel said. She scrunched up her face, thrust her arms out in all directions, and said, "Duh, duh, duh!"

Faye cracked up.

I laughed a little too, to be polite. "Barry's got it," I said.

"You're kidding!" Muriel cried out, smearing her hair over her right eye. "You're kidding!"

"Wow, bummer," Faye said.

I brought them in to see Barry in his crib and in a slow, careful way started to tell them a little bit about his flipping over and his seizures and his snoring.

"Will we see him flip over?" Faye said, sounding repulsed and yet fascinated. She was making it sound like *Barry Gray: The Horror Movie.* Now playing at a theater near you.

"He doesn't flip over anymore," I said. "That only lasted a little while."

"How about a seizure? I want to see that!"

"He's on antiseizure medication."

Muriel stared down at Barry as if he were a squashed pigeon near a curb. "Now he's giving me a funny look," she said. "Like it's me who's the weirdo."

"He can't judge distances," I explained. "So he doesn't know how far away you are."

Just then Barry coughed, spitting up a large, thick, whitish blob.

Faye and Muriel grabbed each other and shrieked.

I got some tissues from the bathroom and wiped off Barry's chin. "He's good at that," I said, utterly humiliated but trying to make a joke out of it. "Well, are you impressed?"

"No!" Muriel said. "I think I'm sick!"

Faye stared at Barry a while longer, realizing Barry wasn't going to do much else besides stare back at her or maybe spit up again. We all went into the living room and sat around, while Faye started in on Topic A. "That new guy, Brendan, is so cool," she said. "I love his bedroom eyes."

I started to laugh. "You mean that kid who's always stoned? He can't keep his eyelids open!"

Fine, I was thinking. We got that over with. I've told them about Barry. And now we can forget about that subject for good.

But the subject of Barry came up again on Monday, when we met up after our last class. I told Faye and Muriel they could come over for pizza that night, and they suddenly fell silent. "What?" I said. "What did I say?" I could feel their silence as if it were heat.

"I'm not allowed to go to your house anymore," Faye said, looking down at the self-inflicted holes in her jeans.

"You're not?" I said.

"My mom doesn't want me hanging around Barry because something might possibly happen."

I swallowed. "Like what, for instance?"

Faye's tone turned a bit nasty. "Like, for instance, he might go into insulin shock."

Muriel nodded.

"He's not a diabetic," I said.

Faye frowned. "What about seizures? You said he had seizures. He might have a seizure!"

"I told you. He's on special medication."

"Look. My mom doesn't want me blamed for anything going wrong with a deformed, sickly child, okay?"

"What about you?" I asked Muriel. I was nearly crying. "Are you barred from the premises too?"

"If you're asking if my parents agree with Mrs. Needleman, I haven't exactly asked them."

78

"Don't bother. I already know their answer."

What was wrong with me? Why should I feel hurt, or angry at them, when I didn't want to be anywhere near Barry, either, not within a million miles?

In late September, New York City got hit by a heat wave. One sweltering, sticky night, Loretta asked me to play "The Flashlight Game" with Barry, and I was too hot to come up with a decent excuse not to.

We turned the lights off. Loretta sat, spread-eagled, on the wooden floor of our living room, while Barry leaned back against her belly, wearing nothing but a diaper. I sat on the couch, holding a flashlight. "Point the flashlight anywhere on Barry's body," Loretta instructed me, "and Barry will rub the area."

"*That's* a game?"

"It can be a lot of fun!"

This made it sound even worse. But I pointed the flashlight at Barry's foot. He looked down at the circle of light for what seemed like an hour, and then touched it.

"Very good, Barry," Loretta said softly. "Go on, rub it, rub the light. Rub your foot."

Barry poked at it, then stared at it, and then flung his hand back in the complete opposite direction.

"Try again," Loretta said.

Barry poked some more, and then looked up at me, letting out a throaty, garbled sound.

"Wonderful, Barry!" Loretta cried. "Did you hear that, El? The beginning of speech. I think he's trying to say your name."

"Oh, brother," I said. Earlier that day, she'd started off a twenty-word familygram to Robert with:

BARRY ALMOST SAID FIRST WORD. SOUNDED
LIKE "ELLEN."

Then she added

HEAT WAVE HERE WOW HOT

and wanted me to supply the last seven words. But I said
my mind was a complete blank. So she finished it off

LOVE, LOVE, LOVE, LOVE, LOVE, LOVE, LOVE.

The "game" continued. I pointed the flashlight at Barry's
leg, arm, belly. Staring, poking, staring, poking. I nearly
fell asleep. "How do you win this game, anyway?" I knew
this had to be some kind of therapy.

"Right now, it's to help Barry feel more connected to his
body. But it's also going to teach him how to wash himself,
when he's older."

Did Loretta have any idea how weird this was, asking
me to help put Humpty Dumpty back together again?

"That's enough," I said, and turned the flashlight off.
Suddenly Barry whimpered. "What's the matter with him?"

"You don't get it, do you?" Loretta said. "He loves you.
He's all relaxed because of you."

"It's his medication," I said.

"He was so rigid when Aunt Beryl was here. Come, feel
his arm."

But I stayed on the couch. "It's too hot to move," I said.

Loretta turned her attention back to Barry. "Barry, you
did so well!" She gave him a hug. "What a good, brave boy
you are."

I went into the kitchen to drink some milk, the only food

80

that didn't jump all around in my stomach. But my hand got shaky and I filled the glass too full. As I stared down at the spreading white puddle on the table, I heard Loretta saying, "These are your ears, Barry. See how I can wiggle them? They can hear me talk to you. This is your mouth. It can taste delicious food."

This is your sister, Ellen. See her stomach? It hurts and hurts.

A week later the heat broke. For several afternoons running, Loretta sat at the kitchen table, dealing with mounds of paperwork from CHAMPUS, the navy's health insurance company. "El, I'm stuck here until dinner," she said each time. "It's so beautiful outside. Please take Barry out in his stroller!"

So I took Barry out in his stroller. It was a special stroller—Barry had to be strapped in very securely, facing whoever was pushing him. Myself, I get dizzy riding backward, but Barry didn't seem to mind it. What did he mind? I wondered.

Ever wheel a baby around? The comments from strangers are endless:

"Isn't he sweet! What's his name?"

"Look at those big baby blues."

"Is he your brother? Aren't you lucky!"

I could take only so much of this. On the way home my last time out, I brushed past an old lady who wanted to ask me all about "the little pumpkin boy."

"He's an abandoned child," I said, "and I'm wheeling him back to the orphanage."

CHAPTER

6

In October, at Grandmother Anne's urging, Aunt Beryl drove into the city one Saturday and brought my grandparents over for a visit.

Aunt Beryl arrived in black—shoes, panty hose, wool skirt, turtleneck sweater, shawl. She air-kissed Barry, but gave me a real kiss, whispering hotly into my ear, "The ride over here was horrid. Anne wouldn't stop talking about Barry. I had to bite my tongue the whole way."

"What are you two whispering about?" Grandmother Anne wanted to know, in her rather deep voice.

Aunt Beryl just stood there.

"Boys," I said quickly.

Grandmother Anne has broad shoulders, a large, thick waist, and sturdy legs like logs. She also has Robert's icy blue eyes, or should I say Robert has hers?

"Boys," Grandmother Anne said, waving them all away. "And speak more loudly, Ellen, so that Mitchell can hear you. He's deaf as a post, you know." She was wearing an orange leisure suit, similar to the one Aunt Beryl had worn on her last visit. Did Aunt Beryl buy it for her, or take her shopping? Was that something you did for your sister's mother-in-law? "Now, where's my little honey bunny?" Grandmother Anne said.

Barry was in Loretta's arms. Grandmother Anne stood over him, oohing and ahhing awhile. Grandfather Mitchell—he's short, thin, and nearly bald, with a fringe of brown hair around his large ears—gazed at Barry in silence. "He looks tired," he said quietly. "He looked that way before. Loretta, is he always tired?"

Loretta flinched slightly, as Aunt Beryl shot looks at her.

"Barry just woke up," I said loudly. "He'll be his perky self again in a minute." Aunt Beryl wasn't the only one who didn't want to talk about Barry's cerebral palsy.

Loretta suggested we go into the kitchen, where she'd spread out a buffet of cold cuts, German potato salad, and fresh onion rolls from the bakery downstairs. We all filled paper plates, and went back to the living room. Grandmother Anne sat beside Loretta and Barry on the couch, with Aunt Beryl and Grandfather Mitchell on either side in easy chairs.

I sat opposite in the rocking chair. I ate two bites of a roll, and then had to stop. Hard to believe I used to crave chili dogs heaped with onions, enchiladas smothered in green sauce, Szechuan chicken with sweet and hot peppers. I fetched a half gallon of milk, and kept it on the floor right beside the rocking chair, pouring myself a glass whenever I felt a pang of hunger.

"My grandson is precious, Loretta," Grandmother Anne said, stroking Barry's arms. "Goodness, he's got muscles already!"

Loretta gave me a tiny wink.

"Won't Barry make the girls swoon when he's a handsome

football star!" Grandmother Anne went on. "Football can help Barry get into Yale. I wonder what he'll be after that? Perhaps a brilliant lawyer, maybe a surgeon."

Aunt Beryl glanced at me, quite pale. *See? See how I have to bite my tongue?*

Grandfather Mitchell was watching the way Loretta carefully placed both of Barry's legs around one of hers. "One step at a time," he said. "Let's see how Barry gets along in the world before we enroll him in medical school."

Grandmother Anne waved him away. "I wonder what Barry's first word will be," she said. "I hope it's 'Grandma,' " she added wistfully.

I heard George and Gracie coming downstairs for a walk, and wished I were going with them, even if I had to be a dog myself. As I poured out another glass of milk, Grandfather Mitchell said to me, "That'll be your fifth. One more after that and you'll turn into a cow."

Everybody smiled at his joke. Something behind his liquidy brown eyes told me he was thinking about how Ellen was getting along in the world too.

"Moo," I remarked.

On a cool, breezy Sunday afternoon a couple of weeks later, I walked around Soho with Faye and Muriel. All morning Loretta had kept talking to me about staying home that day and spending time with her and Barry. Her voice sounded so urgent. That tone was something she seemed to have picked up in the last few days. I'll have to keep an eye on her, I thought. Maybe she's getting weird again.

Faye and Muriel were talking about . . . what else? The Boy of the Month.

"Perry had a hickey," Faye said, chewing gum and cracking it so loud it sounded like a miniature fireworks show was going off in her mouth. "And was he ever flaunting it! He could've worn a turtleneck."

"It was Lorelei," Muriel said. "She's such a tramp. She's been chasing Perry like crazy."

"I'm sure it's the other way around," I said. "After all, she's your basic definition of gorgeous."

"She's ugly!" Muriel spit out. "She's got thunder thighs."

"Not only that," Faye said, "but her eyes aren't even. One is higher than the other."

"You're kidding!" Muriel was suddenly fascinated.

"Hold up a ruler and see for yourself," Faye told her.

"I will!" Muriel said.

Maybe this was why Muriel kept one eye hidden. It didn't sound so terrible to me. I remembered reading somewhere that Rita Hayworth had been the same way. But Rita Hayworth didn't let it stop her.

We walked slowly past stores with overflowing bins of clothing out front, and dozens of street vendors with table displays full of earrings, makeup, socks, gloves, sweaters, books, batteries—basically, you name it.

"Oh, I love these earrings!" Faye cried, bending over a glittering display. "But I don't have any money."

"Me, neither," Muriel said. "I'd die for this lipstick. Look, it's green, but it's supposed to turn into 'your perfect color' when you put it on."

I bought four star-shaped earrings and gave them to Faye. I bought a green lipstick and gave it to Muriel. Poor Muriel—the lipstick seemed to erase her lips completely.

So why did I spend my last twelve dollars on gifts for Faye and Muriel? I wasn't sure, exactly, especially since I'd stopped feeding the cookie jar. Maybe it had something to do with feeling that the price of friendship went up when you had someone like Barry for a brother.

Coming around a corner, we found a cluster of people blocking our way. I walked up behind a woman in a kerchief and asked, "What's going on?" But she didn't turn around. Peering over her shoulder, and over a couple of other people's shoulders, I saw the reason for the cluster.

A boy. About ten years old. All by himself. Wearing a brown cap with flaps pulled way down over his ears and a gray tweed overcoat that looked like it belonged to an old, old man. In his fist he held a string attached to a bright blue balloon. He had a round, moon-shaped face, and he was shouting. "Balloony!" he kept saying, in a thin, screechy, hoarse voice. Over and over again.

"You said it, kid," somebody called out. "You're balloony, all right."

"Leave the poor child alone!" somebody else said.

"Hire the handicapped!" a voice shouted from somewhere behind me. "They're fun to watch!"

I heard a ripple of giggling. I huddled inside my down jacket.

"Does anybody know this child?" said the woman in the kerchief. "Does anybody know his mother?"

Muriel clicked her tongue. "You'd think his mother would keep a retard like him at home," she muttered to me.

"Balloony!" the boy shouted again.

Ten years from now, that might be Barry. Ten years from now, Loretta might have to rescue him from inside a cluster of people. Or maybe I would have to walk through the crowd and take his hand. I'm his sister. The Balloony Boy is my brother.

I heard laughter close by, filling my ears. Must be Faye or Muriel. Right in my ears.

The woman in the kerchief spun around. She had large

black eyes, like a gypsy. "We're waiting for the boy's mother!" she snapped at me.

"What are you telling me for?" I said. But I knew. That laughter. It was coming out of me. I was still laughing.

"This isn't like you," Faye said.

Was it? I honestly didn't know. I'd never laughed at a retard before. But if you do something, it must be because you're the type of person to do it.

"Let's get out of here," I said.

"Well, where are we going now?" Muriel asked.

"Paper Moon." I knew that inside my favorite store I could feel like a different type of person.

As we crossed the street, a woman rushed by us. She wore a long tan coat; she had a moon-shaped face; her eyes were wide and frantic and pale blue. It had to be the Balloony Boy's mother, rushing to his rescue.

Just inside Paper Moon, I took a deep breath, filling my lungs. It smelled of cedar. For a moment, I shut my eyes and felt surrounded by dense woods. Lace covered the walls of the store from top to bottom, and wind chimes spilled out sweet, delicate sounds. There were graceful brass bracelets for sale, and floating candles, and hand-painted silk scarves, and necklaces with bright stones, and kimonos, and geodes—plain dull rocks on the outside, but when they're cut in half, you can see that they're lined with shockingly beautiful crystals on the inside, sparkling jagged peaks of silver and white.

Muriel tried on a brass bracelet. "I love this," she said. "It's a little tight, though."

"This necklace would look great on me," Faye said, holding up a silver chain dotted with black stones.

What I wanted was a geode. I'd never wanted anything so much. I knew I had to have it.

Geodes cost money, a thin, screechy, hoarse voice said in my head. And you turned your money into earrings and lipstick! So you can't have a geode, can you?

It was the Balloony Boy, saying these things to me, laughing at me, getting back at me. Well, I could show him how wrong he was.

I looked around. There was only one person taking care of the whole store, a woman with long, silver-white hair. She was talking to a customer up at the cash register. Several other customers wandered around, murmuring to each other, and someone wearing a brown coat was standing near the door and looking out the window, as if waiting for somebody. I felt blood rush to my face.

"Ellen looks scary," Muriel said. "Like she has a fever."

I grabbed two halves of the same small geode, and slipped them both into the right pocket of my jacket.

"Are you nuts?" Faye said.

"Shh!" I whispered. "Don't let her catch me." I motioned toward the woman with the silver-white hair.

"This isn't like you," Faye said, for the second time that day.

I was full of surprises.

"I cut school seven days so far," Muriel said. "I can't get into any more trouble."

"Neither can I," Faye said—no reason given.

"So, leave," I said flatly. "If you two are so scared, go ahead. But I was going to get some nice stuff for you too."

"Oh, yeah?" Muriel said.

"Like what?" Faye said.

Soon there was a necklace for Faye and a bracelet for Muriel in my left pocket.

"Let's go," I said.

Faye and Muriel headed out of the store first. Just as a

rush of cold air hit my face, I felt a hand on my arm, gripping it tight, even through my jacket. My first thought was, there'll be fingerprint marks there later, I know it. The hand grabbing me belonged to a bearded man in a brown coat. The one I thought had been waiting for somebody.

I nearly twisted my neck, looking for Faye and Muriel. But they'd disappeared.

"Come with me," the man said. I smelled hot dog and melted cheese and sauerkraut on his breath. He led me through the store; the edges of my vision got blurry; I walked straight ahead very carefully so I wouldn't step into the blur. Then I was in a small, dim room in the back.

This room was nothing like the rest of Paper Moon. No chimes, no lace, no smell of cedar. Only peeling paint, a bulb hanging from the ceiling, a scratched-up wooden desk, and two office chairs on either side of the desk. There were rips in the red plastic covers of the chairs, exposing fluffy white padding.

The bearded man told me to sit down.

The woman with the silver-white hair came in and sat down in the other chair. She was wearing a flowing dark red skirt and a white turtleneck. She looked straight into my eyes. There was nowhere else for me to look but straight back into hers. Then she leaned her right elbow on the desk, and began scooping her right hand toward herself, as if to say, come on now, put the stuff up here, all of it. I couldn't help noticing that even in harsh light my geode looked stunning.

"Thank you, Greg," she said, not taking her eyes off me. "Watch the store while I deal with this one, okay?"

Greg left.

"Don't tell me you merely forgot to pay," she began, flinging her hair back. "Don't tell me your friends put those things in your pockets. Don't tell me you didn't even know about it. Don't tell me it's your first time and you won't ever do it again."

I won't ever do it again! I wanted to say. It is my first time! I froze up. She'd never believe me. If I were her, I wouldn't believe me, either. Tears began to stream down my face.

"How old are you?"

"Twelve and a half," I managed to say.

"Well, then, you're old enough to hear this, not that it will do any good. People like me have to work for a living, and we work hard. I've got three kids, and I'm the one taking care of them, nobody else. I work here all day, and then I go straight home to make the scarves at night. You understand why I've got no patience for kids like you, why I never want to see you in my store again?"

I kept on crying.

"If you were older, I'd call the police. All I can now is call your parents. Let's have your number. Let's tell Mommy and Daddy what Baby's been up to."

I gave her my number. Then she left me alone in the dim room. I was so tired. My bones felt tired. I wanted to sleep for a whole year, and then wake up with no pain.

Loretta came to pick me up, wheeling Barry in his stroller. The woman with the silver-white hair was smiling at Barry—and she had a terrific smile, warm and real. I felt an ache as I realized that I might have liked her, and she might have liked me—if I hadn't stolen from her.

"Let's go home," Loretta said, and didn't say another word for an hour.

On the street, her silence wasn't so bad. At home, it was unbearable.

Loretta put Barry to bed, and ironed a few blouses, and

sat on the couch reading the orange book—and the whole time I kept waiting for her to say something to me, to say *anything*.

"Listen, Mom," I pleaded, standing in front of her. "Remember how you felt when eleven doctors wouldn't believe you? Well, the woman in *Paper Moon* wouldn't believe me, either. I mean, she talked so much I never had a chance to explain. I was holding that stuff for Faye and Muriel—"

"Oh, Ellen, stop it!" This wasn't the response I was looking for—a sigh of relief, plus a hug. "I might have believed you. I might have believed that those girls tricked you into it somehow. But not after what happened last week. I wasn't going to mention it, but now you're getting worse."

"Mention what?" I felt panic fill my throat. "What happened last week?"

"Ms. Stapler called me. She said you'd failed your fourth test in communications class. She wanted to know how you were bearing up at home. She kept apologizing for calling during such a traumatic time. I said, 'Ms. Stapler, whatever are you talking about?' And she said, 'Mrs. Gray, I'm so very sorry about your divorce.' "

I just stood there. What else could I do? My eyes were all cried out. They actually felt dry.

"I assured Ms. Stapler there was no divorce. She was stunned and deeply upset. She told me she felt her own feelings were being used against her. She couldn't understand why you would do such a thing. I couldn't, either, but I told her that maybe this had something to do with Ellen's brother—"

"You didn't tell her about Barry!"

"Of course I did. And she was willing to excuse you then. But I still didn't know what to think."

"You didn't have to tell a complete stranger about Barry, just because I lied a little!"

"But now it's stealing too."

There's also cheating on math tests, I thought, if you're making a list. "Maybe I'm a rebel," I said. "You once told me you were a rebel, a long time ago."

"I never stole. I don't believe I ever lied."

"So punish me," I said. "Make me stand in the corner. Put me on bread and water. Lock me in my room and never let me out!" Suddenly I stood very still. I did want to be punished. I was almost begging for it.

Loretta looked as if she might start to cry. "I can't . . . punish you, Ellen. I don't want you angry and resentful. I want you to learn. Robert will be home soon. Maybe he'll know what to do." She went back to the orange book. Her silence pulled at my heart.

I went into my room and lay down on my bed. Several minutes later, Loretta was standing in my doorway.

"Are you getting hungry?" she asked me. "What do you feel like having?"

Milk. Just milk.

Robert came home in November. After a long, whispery, head-to-head with Loretta on his first night, he came into my room and said, "Ellen, I want to talk to you."

It was cold and blustery outside. He looked all dressed up, even in a turtlenecked sweater and wool pants. But then he also looked formal in pajamas. After taking a long, deep breath, he said, "Your behavior of late is not the issue. What is most important is what's causing your behavior. Loretta and I feel that if you were made to understand your own state of mind, your behavior would change."

My own state of mind. I wondered if he had any idea what that was.

"Loretta and I think you are going through profound grief."

"Grief?" I said.

"Let me try to explain it." A vein stuck out in his forehead. "It happened to your mother, when Barry was born. You see, when a woman is carrying a baby, she is also carrying something else too, something that is growing inside her, along with the baby. That something is a dream—the dream of a normal, healthy child. When a child is born handicapped, the dream dies. Ellen, you wanted a normal brother or sister. That was your dream. Now you are grieving for the loss of your dream."

"Grieving," I said, trying to sort this out in my mind. Robert never spoke about things like dreams and grief and loss.

"You must finish grieving for your dream and bury it," he told me, "and accept Barry for what he is—a less than perfect child."

I pressed my hands to my stomach. The pain seemed to be getting worse every day. "I didn't . . . want a normal brother," I said. The pain made it hard to get the words out. "So once again your theory . . . is wrong." But he got me thinking, a little brother might have been fun. A little brother who wasn't the Lump.

"We are all adjusting to this, Ellen. We must sharpen our wits and widen our hearts. I'll help you any way I can."

You're leaving again next month! How can you help?

"If you need to talk to a psychiatrist, that can be arranged."

"It hurts," I whispered. "It hurts."

"I know," he said softly, his voice close by. I smelled strong black coffee on his breath.

"No, my stomach . . ."

"Ellen, honey, no excuses, please."

"Daddy, I'm sick, really and truly sick."

He looked at me, hard. Then he said, "Let's get you to a doctor."

There's a doctor in a naval hospital over in Staten Island whom I've seen several times since we moved to New York. He's got bright red hair, and his office is splattered with pictures of his six redheaded kids and two Irish setters.

A quick phone call, a cab ride, an examination on a cold metal table, a tablespoon full of thick white liquid that tasted like melted rubber. Then the four of us sat in plush leather chairs in the doctor's office that night, all those redheads staring down at us.

"Ellen's got a preulcerous condition," the doctor told us cheerfully. He was always cheerful, as far as I knew.

"A preulcerous condition," Loretta said, bouncing Barry very lightly in her lap. "What does that mean?"

"It means that Ellen is getting herself an ulcer."

Loretta put her hand to her mouth. "But she's so young!" she said. "Poor baby," she added.

"What's an ulcer?" I said. "I mean, I've heard of them." They made me think of bald men with beer bellies.

The doctor chirped in, "It's when the stomach begins to digest the lining of the stomach wall. In other words, the stomach starts to eat itself."

It made me sick just to hear it!

The upshot was, from now until the end of December I had to take the medicine three times a day, eat only bland foods, and rest in bed.

94

"Two whole months in bed!" I complained in the cab going home. "I've simply got to have a chili dog. And that medicine—it's vile!"

Between complaints I took some deep breaths. I had to admit, the medicine didn't have an aftertaste. And I'd been eating only bland foods, anyway. And a long bed rest actually sounded tempting. And I didn't want to feel sick for the whole rest of my life.

The next day Loretta called my teachers, and they all said I could catch up on my homework in January. Christmas break was coming up soon, so I wouldn't be missing much school, after all.

And so began my quarantine.

7

Is there anything more boring than being sick and waiting to be not sick? It was one thing to like the idea of resting in bed, and another to actually do it. I slept a lot those first few weeks, but then I was awake all day. Once my stomach started feeling better, I yearned for something so spicy it would turn my hair red, but all I could eat was oatmeal, rice, mashed potatoes, skim milk, and baked chicken. So who needs teeth? Day after day after day, all I could do was sleep or read or watch TV, and when I got out of bed or off the couch, and started wandering around the loft in a flannel nightgown and furry slippers, all I had to look at was Barry.

And Barry at ten months was the ultimate answer to the question, What could be more boring? Barry, on Loretta's lap, loudly gulping his milk; Barry, wrapped in a Snugli and drooling; Barry, in his crib, snoring like a chainsaw (a new one to add to his collection). The Lump That Gulps. The Lump That Drools. The Lump That Snores. And when he gets older, what will he become? The Even Bigger Lump. My stomach no longer felt like it had needles jabbing into it, but even when I just lay in bed, all calm and still, it felt like my insides were jumping around and throwing a party—and I wasn't even invited to it.

We had our usual three-foot-high Christmas tree that Robert, home one weekend, covered with tiny, multi-colored lights, and it sat in its usual spot on the coffee table. When I was little, I used to help him with the lights, and I remembered the thrill of seeing them all click on at once. It felt like waking up inside, when you didn't even know you'd been asleep. Now it was just a boring old tree, and not only that, it got needles all over the floor.

I've always loved our wooden floors, which creaked in a loud and friendly way, as if talking to you. But in the spring Loretta was going to smother them with extrathick carpeting, because, she explained, Barry might be walking soon, and he'll be falling a lot because his balance is so bad. Also, she was going to get rid of our coffee table, and push the soft furniture, as she now called our couch and easy chairs, back against the walls, so Barry wouldn't bump into them. She wanted to give away the rocking chair, but I could never let that happen—it was going in my room, even if the space was too narrow for any actual rocking. A big wall unit was going to replace the TV table on wheels and the stereo cabinet. Loretta got annoyed when I said, "Why don't we all move to a padded cell?"

Christmas was sort of canceled, on account of my illness, but I got some gifts, anyway. Loretta gave me a silver necklace with an amethyst. I was pretty sure she'd bought it at Paper Moon, months ago—it was a little too similar to the one I'd tried to steal for Faye. Aunt Beryl gave me a yellow blouse. I look ill in yellow. Grandmother Anne gave me a wrapped present I recognized immediately as some-

97

thing I'd given her a couple of years before, which she'd never even opened—a sturdy leather belt with a brass buckle. Grandfather Mitchell slipped a twenty-dollar bill inside a card. The most peculiar gift came from Robert—a simple, off-white, nothing-much-to-it lambs' wool turtleneck. It was way too old for me! It was like something I'd see on Ms. Stapler!

One afternoon, between Christmas and New Year's, I was alone in the loft, mourning the fact that I was still sandwiched between flannel sheets and couldn't go outside into what was obviously a gorgeous day—mild, bright, and clear. Loads of pale yellow sunshine streamed in my window, throwing big blocks of light across the bed. Even the traffic sounded cheerful, the rumble of cars over the bumpy street down below. Loretta was out grocery shopping— with Barry, since I explained I couldn't be his baby-sitter, not with a preulcerous condition.

When Loretta got home, she called out excitedly, "Ellen, look who I've got with me!"

She sounded so tickled I thought maybe a puppy had followed her back. But it wasn't a puppy. When I got out to the living room, I found a lady about Loretta's age, but taller, almost six feet, and big without being fat. She wore a button-down-the-front sweater that reached her knees, all gold and maroon and burnt orange, and a wide black lizard belt around her waist. She wasn't pretty, exactly, but stunning anyhow, with enormous round dark eyes and thick black eyelashes, and the kind of high cheekbones you usually see on skinny models. She had a wide, full mouth covered with bright crimson lipstick, and masses of dark red frizzy hair that sprayed out over her shoulders.

And there I was, in my nightgown and slippers, and my hair so dirty it practically stuck to my head and neck.

"Hi, Ellen!" this lady beamed at me, and swung her arm out to shake my hand. I shook hers back. She had a deep, throaty voice, and smelled like wildflowers. "Say, she's a pretty one! You feeling better, honey?"

Usually I didn't like it when strangers called me "honey." But this time it sounded okay.

"I'm getting better, I guess," I answered.

"Good!" she said, and gave my shoulder a squeeze. Who was this lady, and why did she feel like somebody I'd known for years?

"This is Mrs. Maribeth Ramsey," Loretta said, her arms full of Barry, who was squirming. The Lump That Squirmed. "She manages an art gallery downtown."

"Way downtown," Maribeth said. "In Tribeca."

Tribeca stands for the *Tri*angle *Be*low *Ca*nal Street. It's a great, friendly place, and still has more warehouses than boutiques. The way Soho used to be. "What kind of art?" I asked her.

Maribeth grinned at me. She had big dimples. "What kind do you like?" she said.

"Oh, I don't know," I said truthfully, never having thought about it. But then a light clicked on, and I realized I *did* know: "Realistic stuff. I like paintings that are so focused and vivid you'd swear you were looking at photography."

Maribeth thought about this a moment. "I've got it!" she said, and her whole face brightened. "In February I'm exhibiting a young fellow from Czechoslovakia. His work is crisp and alive. You're invited to the opening—you'll come, won't you?"

I was thrilled. It sounded utterly glamorous. Immediately I saw myself there, sipping wine (Loretta allowed me a few sips occasionally), holding a skinny brown cigarette (not smoking it, of course), and discussing art ("It's absolutely brilliant, even more real than photography, don't you agree?"). The only problem with the image was that I was wearing an off-white, lambs' wool turtleneck. And Faye and Muriel were nearby, making fun of everything, ruining it. And Barry was there too. He was always there.

"Of course, you might be busy that night," Maribeth said, her expression softening. "We'll keep it open." She could see instantly that something was wrong—and be really nice about it too. The opposite of Faye and Muriel.

Loretta led us into the kitchen, where she put the kettle on. I noticed her hair looked longer, now brushing past her shoulders. And it was so clean and yellow and sparkling in the sunshine. You could've put my hair in a can and sold it as motor oil. She had on a sweatshirt I liked, white with a black stripe around the collar, and blue jeans. She looked a bit tired, especially her eyes, but these days she seemed more . . . real, somehow, more *Loretta*. If only she didn't always have Barry in her arms. I pushed away the thought that maybe having Barry in her arms had something to do with it.

"I love this kitchen!" Maribeth said, adjusting herself on a high wooden chair. "Yellow walls, my favorite! And what is that heavenly smell?"

"It's the bakery downstairs," I said, sitting down too and kicking off my slippers—even in winter, with the window open, the kitchen was always warm.

"It's like you're in a room where the walls are made of freshly baked bread," Maribeth said.

Loretta and I couldn't help glancing at each other at that one, and we nearly laughed. Maribeth was a wacky one, no doubt about it.

"I'll have coffee with four teaspoons of sugar," Maribeth said. "Isn't that disgusting?"

By Maribeth's third cup of coffee, and twelfth teaspoon of sugar (I was sipping milk, and Loretta was still on her first cup of almond tea), I learned that Maribeth's dark red hair wasn't natural: "It's henna, honey—my real color is somewhere between squirrel and chipmunk"; that she was expelled from a Catholic girls' school for smoking cigarettes: "Me and my two best friends, honey, don't you ever start"; and that she married her husband one week after meeting him: "My father always walked around the house in his underwear. And here was a man in a real suit and tie and *cuff links*! I married the man because he wore cuff links!"

When the groceries were delivered, Maribeth scurried about, helping us put everything into cabinets with fast sweeps of her arms. Of course, she didn't know where the stuff was supposed to go, and she didn't ask. For weeks afterward, Loretta wailed, "Where's the ketchup? Where's the baking soda? Whatever happened to our Unscented Bounce Free?"

"Mom, how did you find—I mean, where did you meet Maribeth?"

"Right near the Peek Freans, my weakness," Maribeth said. "I saw Loretta handling Barry, so I knew right away—"

"Knew what?" I said. Immediately I felt a twinge in my stomach. It always led to Barry. "What did you know?"

"I saw Loretta handling Barry," Maribeth repeated. When she saw my blank expression, she explained, "Handling is a technical term. It means positioning a child with

101

cerebral palsy so he doesn't fall or hurt himself. I know all about it because I have a son with cerebral palsy."

"You do?" I practically gaped at her. Maribeth was sophisticated and offbeat, and cerebral palsy was neither.

"Sam is fifteen," Maribeth said, rolling her eyes. "He's got all those teenage hormones churning around inside him, and he takes everything out on me. What a pain in the butt he is! Sometimes when he comes home, I don't even want to let him in!" She finished her fourth cup of coffee, and gazed at me for several long moments. "It's okay," she said. "I'm allowed to complain about Sam. I'm allowed to hate the way he is sometimes. I'm allowed to be proud of his accomplishments and disgusted by all the work it takes to achieve those accomplishments. And I'll tell you what else I hate—his disability. I always have and I always will." That was when I heard anger in Maribeth's voice. Years of it.

Maribeth pulled a lipstick out of her pocket and used her reflection in our toaster to apply it. My insides started dancing to their own crazy music. I could never admit to anyone that I hated Barry himself. My wish come true— the Lump.

"You're allowed too," Maribeth said simply.

I sat up very straight, as if balancing a book on my head. "Allowed what?"

"To feel whatever it is you're feeling, no matter how bad or ugly or horrible."

"I don't feel bad," I said. But it didn't sound too convincing, coming from a twelve-year-old girl with a preulcerous condition.

Loretta got up, saying she wanted to "put Barry down for his nap." That phrase has always sounded to me like "putting the cat to sleep."

After Loretta left, Maribeth said, "Don't be ridiculous. Of course you feel bad. Why shouldn't you?"

I squirmed around a little. "It isn't a matter of *should* or *shouldn't*. I simply don't."

Maribeth gave me an oh-come-on look. "Really, Ellen," she said, as if we'd been arguing about this for weeks.

Then there was a silence, like a huge, gaping pit. I felt I had to fill it up with words. "But, well, let's just say, for instance, that somebody wanted for a tiny moment for something bad to happen, well, maybe prayed for it to happen, and then something bad actually did happen. That might make somebody feel bad, right?" I couldn't believe I'd said this out loud. I couldn't believe the earth wasn't caving in.

Maribeth smiled. "That somebody had nothing to do with it, honey," she said. "That somebody's just not that powerful. If I ever met her, I'd say, hey, you've got some ego!"

I looked at my hands. They were warm with sunlight. I breathed in deeply, and felt my lungs fill up.

Loretta came back. She began talking, but I wasn't listening, only watching her lips move. When I tuned in again I heard her say, "I've often wondered if it was my fault. Barry was inside my body, after all. My sister Beryl kept telling me I must've fallen when I was pregnant, or must've worried the whole time, or maybe there was something on my husband's side of the family that we didn't know about. I know I'm still confused about the exact cause of Barry's cerebral palsy, and I hope I'll be able to pinpoint it someday, but that's no reason for my sister to make me feel irresponsible, ashamed. She even convinced me not to tell my mother-in-law that Barry is handicapped. Beryl said it would kill her."

"Oh, aren't relatives wonderful?" Maribeth said, rolling her eyes again. "Take it from me. Don't keep it a secret—from anybody."

Loretta nodded slowly. "You're right," she said. "El, let's go see your grandparents very soon, and tell them what we've known for months now, that Barry has cerebral palsy."

Maribeth laughed. She had a loud laugh, the kind that probably annoyed people in movie theaters. "When Sam was born, my in-laws doused him with holy water," she said. "They're still waiting for a miracle!"

A miracle. You had nothing to do with it, Maribeth had said. You're just not that powerful. I cupped my hands, holding the light.

Maribeth stayed until dark. When Loretta woke Barry up and fed him, he gulped loudly and spit up all over himself. Maribeth didn't look disgusted, the way the handsome man and his date had when we all ate in the Italian restaurant. She even helped clean him up, and smiled when she said, "Loretta, did you ever think Barry was choking to death?"

"Constantly!" Loretta answered. She'd never told me that. "But it's worse at night. Barry snores, and when I don't hear the snoring, I can't help thinking that he's suffocated."

I'd never known that, either. I didn't feel like somebody's daughter at that moment, or like a kid meeting her mother's new friend. We were just three people, talking.

Maribeth mentioned a parents' group she belonged to that was going to start meeting again after the holidays, on Thursday nights, to discuss the problems of raising handicapped children. Loretta said it sounded great, but she couldn't leave Barry.

"I'll watch him," I said. Loretta blinked at me. It was the

first time I'd ever offered to do anything for Barry. "I mean, he doesn't do much, right? It's not exactly a tough job."

"Fine, El," Loretta said softly, and hugged her arms.

"So, that's settled," Maribeth said, slapping the table. "When are you going to offer me some food? I could eat the toaster."

"How about some Peek Freans?" Loretta said. "Danish butter cremes sound okay?"

"Yum," Maribeth said.

Before going to sleep that night, I went into my parents' room, to take a peek at Barry. He was snoring loudly, but he was so tiny and thin, in a blue terry-cloth sleeper. His slightly pudgy cheeks had the faint glow of an almost-ripe peach. "Your sister's got some ego," I told him. "And you . . . you don't seem to have any ego at all."

Loretta still went to UCP all day with Barry, but she began working part-time in the late afternoons at the library, while I kept an eye on him. It didn't interfere with my life too much—at this point, it wasn't much of a life.

Robert came home for a brief last visit before his next patrol. This time Loretta didn't cry the first night he was away. I didn't hear any sounds coming from her room, except for Barry.

On New Year's Eve, we watched the ball come down in Times Square on TV, and then it was a whole other year.

Back in school, I wore my lambs' wool sweater. I was all better, and my stomach was back to just being a stomach, something I didn't have to think about.

There'd been some changes at Peter Minuit Junior High. Masking tape had been placed down the center of every hall, in a useless attempt to organize traffic. A lot of kids were wearing rainbow-colored sneakers. A mysterious new dish had been added to the cafeteria menu—health loaf. It was the middle of the school year, but it felt like my first day.

I told Ms. Stapler I was okay now. She looked into my eyes—behind my eyes was how it felt—and said she was glad. Then she gave me enough homework to keep me occupied until I was thirty.

At lunchtime, I went outside to the school yard. Everybody did. There had to be practically a hurricane or a hailstorm to keep the kids inside. Today, the sky was only gray and heavy with low clouds. I stood at the chain-link fence, which served as a kind of zoo cage wall between us and the world across the street—a video store, two clothing boutiques, and a falafel place.

Faye and Muriel caught up with me. They'd called a few times over the break, but each time I'd told Loretta I was too sick to talk. Somehow a preulcerous condition and Faye and Muriel didn't go together—like swimming and eating.

"Look, she's alive," Faye said, narrowing her eyes. "What'd you have so bad you couldn't even come to the phone—AIDS?"

Muriel laughed. She'd gotten a haircut over the break. Except for a clump hanging over her right eye, now her hair stuck up in short, hard, wet spikes all around her face, making her look like a deranged dandelion.

"Or maybe you were in prison," Faye said. "For stealing. What's the deal now—you're out on parole?"

"Something like that," I said.

Faye cracked her gum. "So, anyway, you're not sick anymore, right? So, how about coming over later?"

"We're going to talk about Bob Frost," Muriel said, spraying the s. "He's so cute—he's an identical twin."

I knew Bob Frost's brother, sort of. Ray Frost. The guy I used to cheat off of in math. "Twins sound perfect for you two," I said.

"No!" Muriel said. "We both like only Bob! His brother's a drip! And not nearly as cute!"

"But they're identical." I was in this conversation despite myself.

"It's complicated," Faye said. "Bob got all the personality. Ray's a big nothing. So, when are you coming over?" She started jiggling her leg. I think she knew what I was going to say. The sad thing about Faye was, she really wasn't stupid.

"I'm not coming over," I said.

"What?" Muriel said. "Are you still sick? Are you sick and contagious?"

"I'm not sick," I said. "I'm just not coming over."

"But why?" Muriel wailed. "Why!"

Faye snorted. Her eyes might've filled up a little. "Nice sweater," she said. "Looks expensive. Too bad you're too flat-chested for it." She thrust out her own chest. It wasn't much better. Then she grabbed hold of Muriel's arm to lead her away.

"Wait," Muriel said, touching her head carefully. "Ellen, wait, do you like my hair?"

I nodded. The whole friendship had been a big lie. It seemed only right to end it with a final one.

It always stung Loretta to have to ask Aunt Beryl to drive us somewhere—Aunt Beryl was so proud of the fact that she drove and Loretta didn't. Loretta told me that in cars sometimes she had to take long, deep breaths, shut her eyes, and tell herself she was on an ocean liner. It all dated back to the car crash that had killed her parents.

The following weekend, Aunt Beryl drove us up to Washington Heights in her maroon midsize Chevrolet, to see Grandmother Anne and Grandfather Mitchell in the residential home. Loretta sat in the back with Barry, who was strapped into a car seat, and I sat up front with Aunt Beryl, who, as usual, had on her tan driving gloves and her "special driving sunglasses," as she called them, though they looked like plain old tortoiseshell glasses to me.

And she was a terrible driver! She always stopped with a jerk, and when she started up again, it was in a series of little bumpy beginnings. If you could say a car stuttered, that described Aunt Beryl's driving.

Aunt Beryl slammed on the brakes at a yellow light, throwing everybody forward. The drivers behind us loudly honked their disapproval. "They're overly impatient," she said. At the same time she thrust her right arm out in front of my face, as if to save me from hitting the dashboard.

"I'm wearing a seat belt," I told her.

"It's a reflex," she said. "It's involuntary, something I can't help. Maybe there are a lot of things I can't help, all right?"

That remark was strange, even for Aunt Beryl. Also, I noticed, she was a little too dressed up for this outing, in a strawberry-colored silk dress and big pearl clip-on earrings. Loretta and I had on jeans and cotton sweaters. And Aunt Beryl was using a lot of face powder, some of which had already fallen, like dusty snow, onto her collar. She kept glancing at Loretta and Barry in the rearview mirror, which made her driving worse than ever, inviting more and longer honking. "How's he doing?" she said. How's *it* doing, was what it sounded like. "Is he all right? Maybe car rides don't agree with him. I can always turn the car around."

"Barry's fine," Loretta said.

Aunt Beryl coughed, breathing out a smell of spearmint Tic Tacs. "Maybe it's best if Anne doesn't see Barry," she said. "She might realize he has cerebral palsy and get upset."

"But she just saw him a few months ago and didn't suspect anything," I said. "You remember—she predicted he was going to be a football star, and then a brilliant lawyer surgeon."

"Anne might see things differently now," Aunt Beryl said slowly.

Loretta leaned forward. "Why would that be?" she asked.

I looked over at Aunt Beryl. She hadn't mentioned aerobic dancing in months. Her dress was tight around her hips, and there was a little roll of strawberry silk over the seat belt.

"All right, I told her," Aunt Beryl said, swerving the car slightly. "I'm the bad person, the terrible one, the world's worst human being. I told her last night. You never call her, so somebody's got to, so I call her sometimes, all right? I don't have much family, as you well know, and Anne is part of my family too." Then her voice got small and dim. "I couldn't help it," she said. "It just popped out."

"Well, it wasn't supposed to pop out of you," Loretta said. Oh, she was mad. "It was supposed to come from me, today. That's why we're going in the first place! Maribeth was right! And you've probably made it sound as if Barry is a vegetable."

"I did not!" Aunt Beryl cried. "I just made a simple mistake. You talk as if you've never made any kind of mistake in your whole life, and we both know that's not true. Besides, who is this Mary person?"

"My friend," Loretta said, with emphasis.

Aunt Beryl sniffed. "Go ahead, accuse me some more. I know you don't believe me. I told you, I couldn't help it, but if it makes you happy to say cruel things to me . . ."

I gazed out at the cold, cloudless sky. I believed Aunt Beryl. She couldn't help it.

I've always liked going up to Washington Heights. Spanish music played loudly from car radios, fruit stands sold green bananas, even in January, and kids played handball against brick apartment buildings. It was too bad the residential home was a little world of its own and had nothing to do with all this life right outside its door.

We went inside, got a visitor's pass, and took the elevator up to the sixteenth floor. My grandparents have their own small apartment, and you can see their door as soon as you get off the elevator. It's next to a travel poster of a smiling, wide-hipped girl in a hula skirt, telling you to "Come to Hawaii!" This time, right next to her stood Grandmother Anne, scowling at us, blocking her own doorway. She was in a housedress covered with huge, blood red roses, and at her throat there was a brooch with a big pearl. She'd been to the beauty parlor downstairs recently, and now her hair encircled her head like a puffy cloud.

"Don't tell Mitchell!" She was whispering, despite her claim that Grandfather Mitchell was deaf as a post. "I'm not letting you in until you promise! It would kill him!"

I never knew so many relatives who would die from a piece of news. So far, though, Grandmother Anne was still standing.

Loretta shifted from one foot to the other. "I wanted to tell you both, in my own way," she said. "If you'll just let me in—"

Grandmother Anne leaned her head inside the door. "They're late!" she called out. "I'll wait for them by the elevator!" Then she closed the door behind her, leaving us all outside in the hall. It smelled of disinfectant.

"I should think you'd have a lot to say," Grandmother Anne said to Loretta, still whispering, even though the hall was deserted. "After all," she went on, touching her big pearl lightly, "you took all those drugs when you were such a confused young girl. It was bound to catch up with you, sooner or later. I can only thank God that Ellen was born normal."

"But it wasn't my mother's fault!" I cried out. "It couldn't be!" At the same time I was surprised, though not shocked, to learn that Loretta had taken drugs. But how did Grandmother Anne know about it? I was sure Loretta hadn't told her.

A door creaked open across the hall. "Why, hello, Mrs. DeWitt!" Aunt Beryl called out, in a sugary voice. "Oh, I'm sorry, it's Mrs. Castle, of course."

Mrs. Castle nodded at us as she passed by. She was tiny and stooped and adorable, with a big smile and little pink checks. Do you have grandchildren? I asked Mrs. Castle in my head. Would you like another one?

Grandmother Anne was back to whispering threats: "Don't breathe a word of this to Mitchell. He's frail and doing poorly, and this will kill him, do you understand? He must never know that Barry is afflicted." Afflicted. It sounded like leprosy. Then she clasped her hands together and said, "Oh, why has God done this to little Barry?"

Aunt Beryl cast her eyes to heaven. "I'll never understand God," she said.

Loretta rested her hand on my shoulder as we filed into the apartment. I thought about how Loretta didn't like to punish me for things I'd done wrong. Clearly she knew what it was like to make mistakes, and how it felt to have those mistakes thrown back at you.

We sat down on squeaky plastic chairs and ate butter cookies from a box Grandmother Anne had opened not very recently. It was way too warm, and the air was close, and my mouth felt like dust. I said maybe everybody could go outside to the garden, which was behind the residential home. I was thinking about the trees, standing all stark and strong against the winter sky. Grandmother Anne frowned and explained that Mitchell would catch a chill. That was why the windows were closed, she added. But the windows were always closed. Grandmother Anne had this thing about flies coming in.

Reaching for the cookie box, Grandmother Anne asked Barry, "Does Baby want a cookie? An icky, bicky, sticky cookie?"

Loretta shook her head no. "Barry's not ready for solid food," she said politely. "And please don't talk baby talk to him. I want him to learn real words and real sentences."

Grandmother Anne clucked her tongue. "If that isn't the *silliest*," she said, under her breath.

"Here's a real sentence for Barry," Grandfather Mitchell broke in. "His sister's getting prettier by the hour." That made me feel good. He didn't seem all that frail to me.

I looked over at Barry, in his blue quilted playsuit, sitting on Loretta's lap. His eyes weren't the harsh icy blue of Grandmother Anne's, but the soft blue of a summer sky. The same blue I'd chosen for the walls of my bedroom, when we first moved to New York. Barry was moving his legs all around, just to see what they could and couldn't do. And he was taking everything in—Grandmother Anne looming over him in her bloodred dress; the dull crunch of stale cookies; the bumpy feel of the playsuit under his fingers. Maybe he wasn't such a Lump, after all.

"May I hold him?" Grandfather Mitchell asked.

"Of course," Loretta said, handing Barry over.

Grandmother Anne froze, and exchanged identical squints with Aunt Beryl. There was definitely some kind of connection between those two, an attachment far deeper than any family tie, despite the fact that they weren't really related.

Grandfather Mitchell very gently bounced Barry around on his lap, and Barry was laughing a little. Somewhere in the back of my mind I remembered a less-bald Grandfather Mitchell doing the same thing with me. I'd like it too.

"Don't drop him!" Aunt Beryl said urgently. Everybody looked at her. "Well, he mustn't hurt his head," she explained, her cheeks reddening. "I mean, his poor little *head . . .*" She shrugged.

"I'm not raising Barry on fear," Loretta said. "Fear could destroy him."

"More cookies?" Grandmother Anne said. "Aren't they delish? But watch out—they're fattening."

"I like what Loretta said," Grandfather Mitchell announced. "Let the child be a child. Let him climb trees or ride bikes, if he can. And if he skins his knee, you put a Band-Aid on it, and it heals."

Grandmother Anne and Aunt Beryl shot each other another look: *He doesn't understand.* But Loretta smiled gratefully at her father-in-law.

"Well, rain is coming," Grandmother Anne said. "I always feel it in my knee." I looked out the window at the unbroken blue, utterly cloudless sky.

While Aunt Beryl "visited the powder room," as she put it, Loretta and I waited for her by the car. I asked Loretta if I could try on the Snugli and hold Barry. Loretta adjusted it around my neck and waist. I'd never worn one before—they turn any human being into a kangaroo. Tiny and thin as he was, Barry weighed a lot.

"Mom, what was all that about taking drugs?"

Loretta stiffened her shoulders. "I smoked some marijuana, that's all. It was stupid. You learn from your mistakes."

"But how did Grandmother Anne find out?"

"I don't remember," she replied quickly.

This time, I sat in the back with Barry. Driving along, there wasn't much conversation. My mother sat quietly, and Aunt Beryl sighed a lot and popped Tic Tacs.

At the red lights I placed my hand on Barry's belly so he wouldn't feel the car jerking too much. I could hear him sort of whimpering and making little grunting sounds. "Go on," I told him. "Talk. I bet you have lots to say."

Something swirled around in my chest. It felt fast and hot, almost feverish. I remembered seeing a nature documentary on TV all about wolves. A wolf mother stood at the entrance to her den, guarding her cubs from the cameraman filming her. She looked about as serious as it was possible to look—every inch of her, even the air around her, was focused on one thing, keeping those cubs alive!

I looked at Aunt Beryl's dusty collar. I didn't want her spending too much time with Barry. Or Grandmother

114

Anne, either. Barry couldn't afford to be around people who weren't going to accept him exactly as he was, because he had no defenses. Barry needed people who were willing to understand and help him.

Barry needed me.

PART THREE

Wolf Mother

8

"I'll do it," I said. "Just show me once and then I'll do it." At breakfast the next morning, I wanted to be the one who fed Barry.

"Here you go," Loretta said, plopping Barry down in my lap, so that Barry faced me, and sliding a small pillow between his back and the edge of the kitchen table. Barry was wearing a yellow thick cotton suit and enormous white bib that covered his chest and draped over his shoulders.

Barry could hold his head up now. For the past few months he'd been mostly sitting up at mealtimes. I hadn't really seen it—I hadn't noticed that Barry wasn't the same lumpy kid he was eleven months before.

"Every morning," Loretta said, hovering over me, "Barry gets a bowl of oatmeal and a glass of orange juice with a phenobarbital pill in it. Keep his bowl and his juice on a chair next to you so Barry can see what you're doing and not have to crane his neck. Don't forget to put the pill in the juice—"

"I'll do it." Loretta handed me a pill, and I slipped it into the juice. It fizzed a little and dissolved.

"As you feed Barry, talk to him. Tell him exactly what's happening. The spoon has oatmeal on it, and it's going into Barry's mouth—"

"I'll do it," I said. "Barry, look, the spoon has oatmeal on it." He opened his mouth wide. "Look, he's got two teeth!"

Loretta said excitedly, "You mean, two new ones?"

"No, just two altogether." I cleared my throat. "Okay, Barry, the oatmeal is going into your mouth."

"Tell him to close his lips around the spoon. Tell him to swallow. He forgets sometimes—he thinks the food will just fall in, the way it did when I used to tilt his head back."

"All right, I will."

"Try to get him to hold the spoon. He's got quite a good grip. Don't look annoyed, Ellen, it's the only way he'll learn to feed himself someday."

But I was only annoyed with myself. I wished I knew all of this already and didn't need Loretta to tell it to me.

Barry still gurgled and spit up a lot. I could see him trying to swallow, but he had a hard time doing it, and lots of oatmeal ended up on the bib and on the floor.

Loretta smiled at me. "Maribeth's dog always sits right near her son at every meal," she said, "because he knows he'll get lots to eat."

Changing for gym in school that afternoon, I found bits of oatmeal in my shoes.

The whole day had gone by at record speed. It was odd to find that just by concentrating on my subjects, and taking notes and asking questions in class, I could get home that much quicker.

Loretta, Barry, and I sat on the living room floor, and Loretta showed me a bunch of UCP exercises that I could work on with Barry. She told me that the whole point of doing anything with Barry was to open up his senses. "You're trying to let him know he has a mind and a body," she said, "and that he can use both. It's even part of changing his diaper. See, you have to make sure Barry forms a bridge out of his body. Put your hand under his back and hold it up so he can learn how to push his tummy high in the air."

"I see. I'll do it."

"You've got it," she said. "El, don't forget his nap." And then she took off for the library.

I spent the next four hours with Barry. The time went by so fast it wasn't like "time spent," but "time off." There was all this energy inside me, like wind whipping around a street corner. And the whole time I was talking a blue streak.

"Barry, can you stick out your tongue, like this? Okay, you can put your tongue back in now. Put your hand up on the couch. Feel how rough it is? If I move my finger over here, can you follow it with your eyes? Come on, crawl over to me. What a good crawler you are! Boy, I've got a lot of catching up to do with you. Hey, don't crawl backward! Barry, can you say your name? Baahh-reee? Well, 'buh' is getting close, I guess. Let me give you a great big hug. You're so warm and soft. But you feel solid too. There's something solid inside you, Barry."

During his forty-five minute nap, I did some homework.

That night, I fed Barry more hot cereal, but this time with half a banana mushed up in it. Then I gave him a bath in a bright blue, oblong plastic tub in Loretta's bathtub. Barry clapped, and splashed the water, and held the sides as he kicked his legs. He was a high-spirited kid, no doubt about it.

"Here's cool water coming out—feel how cool? Now I'm changing it to warm. See, it's different."

Barry squeezed his pale brown eyebrows together.

"Here's a real treat for you—shaving cream! I'll spray some in your hand. Doesn't that feel funny?"

Barry laughed, rubbing it around his fingers. Then he stuck a finger in his mouth.

"No, it's just for playing!"

I rinsed Barry and dried him off. His skin felt like the softest velvet. Loretta handed me a cotton sleeper that had cowboys and horses all over. I slipped it on, snapping up the collar and all down the legs.

"Every night, we talk about a different part of Barry's body," Loretta said. "We talk, though he probably doesn't understand all the words yet. Little by little, he'll learn. Last night I did feet. I said, don't forget you have feet, Barry, and your feet are connected to your ankles—"

"I'll do it," I said.

Loretta kissed Barry good night and left the room.

I took his hand. "I'm holding your hand, Barry," I said. "You have nice hands with long fingers. Sharp fingernails too. See, your hand is connected to your wrist, and your wrist is connected to your arm, and your arm goes all the way up to your shoulder. All of you is connected. All of you belongs to Barry."

Barry looked up at me with dreamy blue eyes. He grabbed hold of my index and middle fingers. What a grip! He practically cut off the circulation.

"You sleep well now, Barry," I said. And kissed his velvet forehead.

* * *

Over the next few weeks I found out how much fun Barry could be. It felt like a big secret I'd finally been let in on.

Early mornings were fun, because then I could wake Barry up and watch him open his eyes and give me a big smile. He didn't always wake up right away, because the phenobarbital made him really sloopy, and sometimes I had to walk around the loft with Barry curled up over my shoulder, before he was fully awake. But always I got my smile.

Before changing his diaper, I made a puppet out of the new diaper, and made the puppet nibble at his toes. Barry laughed and shrieked.

We sang lots of songs together. "The head bone's connected to the neck bone, the neck bone's connected to the shoulder bone. . . ." I sang way off-key, but did Barry ever complain?

Not all that long ago, Loretta had wanted me to become an "active little baby" for Barry. Back then, it sounded like the worst possible torture. But it was now the best part of the day.

"Hey, let's crawl over to that pencil!" I'd say to Barry, getting down on my knees. "Go ahead, pick it up. Very good. Now let it fall. I'll loosen up your fingers for you. Oh-oh, it's rolling away. Let's crawl over there and catch that runaway pencil!"

I invented a new exercise that gave us something to do even when Barry got tired of being an active little baby. We sat in front of the full-length mirror in Loretta's closet.

"Where's Barry's nose?" I'd ask. "There it is! Look, here are Barry's ears. They can hear me say, you're doing great, Barry. You're growing and changing all the time. You're the best grower and changer I ever saw."

* * *

The last week in January, Loretta brought up the subject of my thirteenth birthday. "Let's have a party," she said at dinner, sounding all excited about it already.

"Barry's birthday is coming up too," I said, feeding Barry some cereal with my right hand while eating a chicken leg with my left. I'd become an expert at feeding two people at every meal. "His birthday's even more important—it's his first. I've already had twelve. Come on, Barry, big swallow."

"But, El, it's a big deal, you're going to be a teenager!"

But it was Barry's birthday that felt like the big deal. One whole year to get used to the place. Now he could really get going. "Why don't we make it a double celebration? We can have a party in the middle of February, between the two birthdays."

"Fine," Loretta said. "I was thinking we could ask Maribeth."

"Yes, definitely," I said. "And can we invite Grandfather Mitchell without Grandmother Anne?"

Loretta rolled her eyes, a habit she'd picked up from Maribeth. "Not a chance. You want Mitchell, you get Anne and Beryl too. With three you get egg roll."

Sometimes she said things like that, and I let them float on by. "Just Maribeth, then," I said.

"How about some of your friends?" Loretta asked. "Who else would you like to invite?"

"Mmm," I said, pretending to be thinking it over. "Let's just keep it small this year."

On a mild-as-April Saturday afternoon in the middle of February, Maribeth burst into the loft bearing a bag over her shoulder, Santa Claus–style. She had on watermelon red lipstick and wore a green V-neck flannel dress that billowed out around her knees. Her hair, clipped back in a wooden barrette, looked like the tail of a comet. She looked terrific. She probably always looked great, even first thing in the morning.

"Oh, balloons!" she cried, gazing around at the walls at thirteen red balloons and one blue balloon, all of them blown up by Loretta. "I adore balloons. Sam hates them. You know that squeaky sound balloons make when you rub them on your hair? It makes Sam crazy."

You mean, it makes Sam balloony, I thought. A word I'd probably never forget.

We pushed the living room furniture together so we could all sit in a close, cozy huddle. Loretta and Maribeth put several gifts on the floor near Barry and me.

Maribeth pointed to a book-size box, beautifully wrapped in glossy red paper and a red satin ribbon. "That's for you," she told me. "Open that one first."

Hugging Barry to my chest in the rocking chair, I leaned over and picked it up. "I practically don't want to open it," I said, already pulling the ribbon. "Oh," I breathed a moment later. Personalized stationery. ELLEN GRAY—tall, elegant, black letters on top of creamy gray paper, and my name and address on all the envelopes. "It's so nice," I said. "It's almost too nice."

"You deserve it, honey," Maribeth said.

I'm not so sure about that, I thought. Wait a minute, I told myself. It's your birthday. It's all right.

The next present was a big white box from Loretta. It was a denim miniskirt from the Gap! Faye's dream come true.

"You'll be a knockout in that," Maribeth said.

It was a beautiful skirt. And if I wanted that kind of thing, it would be exactly what I wanted. But I didn't think I'd be wearing it all that often. It seemed a little young for me.

Loretta handed me a card from Robert, which contained three ten-dollar bills and this message: "Buy anything you desire. So sorry to miss your birthday." One thing I could get with it might be a rubber stamp for him: SO SORRY TO MISS YOUR _____ (fill in the blank).

These were all great gifts, but I wasn't feeling all happy and warm and excited inside. I figured maybe I just wasn't in a gift-getting mood.

But no doubt about it, I was in a watching-somebody-else-get-gifts mood. Tearing into a soft, flat package for Barry from Maribeth, I practically squealed with delight. "Oh, look, Barry, it's a stuffed sheep! Feel its wool, how soft it is."

There was one strange thing about it—the sheep was amazingly flat, as if it had been run over by a truck. It could have been a stuffed flounder. But Barry grabbed it and hugged it and threw his arms around it.

"See?" Maribeth said. "That's why it's made so flat. That way Barry can hug it, and sleep right on top of it. Kids with CP don't like anything too bulky."

"What a terrific gift!" I said. "We love it."

Loretta gave Barry a small brown-and-white plastic cow. "Touch its nose," she told Barry, and as soon as he did, it mooed and swished its tail with a slight clicking sound. Barry and I laughed out loud.

I'd hidden my gift for Barry in my room, behind a closed door. I handed Barry and his cow over to Loretta, went into my room, and walked slowly back with it.

"Ellen, you're a genius!" Maribeth declared.

It was a clear glass tank, with several inches of water inside, and a layer of tiny multicolored rocks—and a big, slow, lumbering, slightly-pissed-off-looking turtle.

"However did you think of it?" Loretta asked, shaking her head and smiling, as if my thinking of it was as big a surprise to her as the turtle itself.

"Well, I wanted a pet for Barry," I began, placing the tank on the floor and settling back into the rocking chair. "But puppies move around way too fast, and a kitten might scratch or bite him. Yesterday I went into Fin 'N' Skin, and there was this turtle. He looked straight at me and yawned. I knew right away he was Barry's turtle."

Loretta and Maribeth looked at the turtle, while I looked at Barry. He was staring and staring and staring. Everything was so completely new for him. But I guess that's true for all babies.

"He needs a name," Maribeth said.

I thought a moment. "Let's wait until Barry can talk," I said, "so he can name his own turtle. And don't worry, Mom, I'll clean out the tank, and feed the turtle, and I'll keep the tank on my bureau."

"I'm not worried," Loretta said, as Barry's turtle closed his eyes slowly and then went to sleep with his head tucked in almost all the way.

Loretta handed out plates of chocolate cake with chocolate icing, and mugs of hot chocolate, and a small dish of banana pudding for Barry. Maribeth ate two slices of cake, and then ran her finger along her plate, scooping up every last speck of chocolate.

"I'd like to make a toast," Loretta said, holding up her

mug. "Here's to Ellen, who's been so wonderful lately. I feel like I'm on vacation. And Barry just adores being with his idol. Cheers—to Ellen!"

I took a big sip of hot chocolate, and sat back with Barry, stroking his thin, straight hair. It was the color of dark, rain-soaked soil.

"It's time for Barry's nap," Loretta said, whisking Barry away before I even had a chance to say, I'll do it.

Maribeth slipped off her shoes, and stretched out her legs luxuriously on the couch. Then she said to me, "Things are different now, aren't they?"

"Different?" I said. "How?"

"When I met you, you hardly looked at Barry. Now you hardly look at anyone else."

I smiled at her. "I guess he's kind of cute," I said.

Maribeth's dark eyes gleamed in the late afternoon winter light. "I wasn't all that worried about you before," she said mildly, "even though you were getting over a preulcerous condition. *Now* I'm beginning to worry."

Sometimes Maribeth made no sense at all. "Has my mother said something to you about me?"

"Only how pleased she is at everything you're doing. She says you're practically Barry's second mother."

I liked the sound of that, but I could see that Maribeth didn't.

"Tell me, Ellen, how are your grades?"

"Never better," I said proudly. This would stop her worrying. "I do all my homework and studying during Barry's naps, and after he goes to sleep. I work really well—I don't even hear his snoring anymore."

"You stay up late sometimes, making sure your homework is absolutely right?"

"Yes," I said, "and it's worth it. My grades have been—"

"Uh-huh, you told me. Ellen, how come I don't see any of your friends over here today?"

I rocked back and forth, back and forth. The floor creaked, loud and friendly. "No particular reason," I said.

She barely had time to hear the answer before asking, "Any idea what you'd like to be when you grow up?"

I stopped rocking and took a deep breath. "No, no idea, as a matter of fact. But I've got some time to think about it, right? I've only been a teenager for two weeks."

Maribeth sat up and leaned so close to me I could see where her watermelon red lipstick ended and her cherry red lip liner began. "Promise me," she said slowly. "Promise me you won't be too perfect."

"Too perfect . . . not too likely in my case!"

"Promise me," she said again.

"All right, I promise," I said. But I didn't know what she was talking about.

The following Friday was the night of the opening of Maribeth's gallery for her Czechoslovakian painter, the party she'd invited me to the day I met her. For the occasion, I put on a below-the-knee navy blue wool skirt, a sturdy leather belt with a shiny brass buckle, and a white cotton blouse, buttoned way up at the neck and also down at the cuffs.

Loretta smiled when she saw me sitting on the couch. "Honey, it's not a visit to the principal's office," she said. "You can wear jeans if you like. Or at least open up your collar and roll up your sleeves."

"I'm quite comfortable," I told her, and she went back

to her room. But really I was the exact opposite of comfortable, and it had nothing to do with my outfit.

Any minute now, a baby-sitter was going to come over. A person I'd never met, a baby-sitter recommended by somebody in Loretta's parent's group—somebody else I'd never met—was going to feed Barry dinner and give him a bath and put him to bed. A total stranger, twice over. I kept folding and unfolding my arms.

When the doorbell rang, I buzzed in the Total Stranger—and had to take a step back at the sight of her.

She had purple hair that fell to her shoulders in a thousand beaded braids that knocked into each other with loud clacks. Purple eye shadow covered her eyelids, and below her eyes there were black, raccoonlike lines. She wore ankle-high black pointy boots, purple leg warmers, bleached jeans, and a huge sweatshirt that said NO PROBLEM.

"Hiya," she said. "I'm Rainbow."

I couldn't even talk. I sort of waved her inside.

"Hey, I like your loft! You probably moved in a long time ago, right, when it was really cheap, and now it's worth like a million dollars?"

"Rainbow," I managed to say. "Is that your real name?"

"Can you believe it?" she said, laughing. "My parents were hippies, back in the old days. My teachers in college can't get into it, though. They call me Renée."

What I couldn't believe was that she was in college. I felt about a hundred years older than her.

"So, where's the kid? He's got CP, right? That's what your mom said. She was so friendly on the phone."

I cleared my throat. "Of course you know how to feed a child with CP," I said carefully.

"Oh, sure!" Rainbow said, laughing again. "You know, in

a lot of ways it's not all that different from feeding a nondisabled baby."

I let that one go by. I'd never fed a nondisabled baby. "Of course you know he gets phenobarbital with dinner," I said.

Rainbow smiled. "What's that?" she said.

I grabbed her arm. "You don't know what phenobarbital is?" Standing so close to her, I noticed a musty smell that seemed a little familiar.

"Just tell me what to do," Rainbow said gently, easing out of my grasp. "I've even given kids insulin injections. Kids trust me."

Suddenly I recognized that smell. A couple of years ago, on the street, I'd walked behind two guy sharing a joint. It was marijuana. Rainbow, Barry's baby-sitter, was stoned! No wonder she kept laughing and smiling, and didn't know what I was talking about.

My heart pounded against my chest. "Listen," I said. "There's been a big mistake. I'm not actually going out tonight. So you can go home now because we don't actually need you."

"What?" Rainbow tossed her braids around, *clackety-clack-clack*. "Your mom especially called me for tonight—"

"She got all mixed up. She gets that way sometimes. How much was she going to pay you?"

Rainbow frowned. "I usually get five dollars an hour."

"Let's see, let's see." I rummaged through my bag and pulled out my wallet. How many hours would it have been? I couldn't figure it out. "Here," I said, handing over three ten-dollar bills. Robert's birthday money. "Well, goodbye."

Rainbow took the money and shrugged. "Can I at least meet the kid? I really do like kids."

"He's taking a nap," I said, which he was. And then I closed the door behind her.

I sat on the couch, and a thought popped into my head: Am I slightly crazy? Well, I told myself right back, was a wolf mother slightly crazy to do everything in her power to protect her den?

A few minutes later, Loretta came into the living room. "Didn't I hear the bell?" she said. "Wow, that perfume! Strong stuff! Where's Rainbow?"

"I sent her home," I said simply.

"You did *what*?"

"You really should thank me," I told Loretta, ignoring the blaze in her eyes. "She was on marijuana. Can't you smell it?"

"Ellen, I don't believe this. That smell is nothing like marijuana, and believe me, I ought to know. It's just some cheap perfume."

I felt my face grow hot. "Well, anyway, she didn't even know what phenobarbital was."

Loretta sighed. "All you had to do was tell her to give Barry some juice. I already put the pill in it."

"She didn't even know Barry," I said in a low voice. "She didn't care about him—how could she?" There was a brief silence. I just sat there, and Loretta just glared at me. "She had purple hair!" I pleaded.

"Sometimes I don't understand you," Loretta said. "Rainbow is supposed to be wonderful with handicapped kids."

But I was still glad I'd thrown her out. Let her go and be wonderful with somebody else's handicapped kids.

"What about tonight?" Loretta groaned. "How can I find another baby-sitter on such short notice?"

"You can still go," I said. "I really should stay home tonight, anyway—I've got lots of homework."

"But you were so looking forward to it!" Loretta said. "And Maribeth was looking forward to having you there."

"It's better this way," I said, already loosening my belt and unbuttoning my blouse.

After I put Barry to bed, I sat at my desk and stared down at a piece of creamy gray paper with my name at the top. "Dear Maribeth," I began. "I'm really sorry that I missed your opening. But Barry needed me, and I couldn't let him down. I'm not ever going to let Barry down."

But instead of mailing it, I crumpled it up and threw it away.

Lots of different things changed all at the same time, just after the beginning of March.

The whole living room looked as if it had been spun wildly, like a centrifuge, until every object in it got flattened against the room's edges, leaving a big, empty space in the middle. Our couch and easy chairs were lined up along the wall opposite the windows, like the obedient furniture in a doctor's waiting room. The beautiful, creaky wooden floor got covered in blue carpet so spongy and thick that it squished up between your toes when you walked barefoot on it. Between the windows, a wall unit with a brown-and-white marbled veneer held the TV, VCR, and stereo. Actually the TV and everything else looked trapped, like prisoners in some kind of furniture-appliance war. So watching TV from the couch felt like sitting in the last row at the movies. Aunt Beryl took the coffee table home, and I got the rocking chair, which was now wedged in next to my bed.

Robert came home that same first week in March. For his arrival, Loretta dressed Barry up in a tiny sailor's suit. I wasn't too crazy about turning Barry into a little prop.

133

Somehow I felt better when Barry flinched at his first sight of Robert. It makes sense, I thought. Kids are supposed to be scared of strangers, and Robert was practically a stranger.

When I put Barry to bed that night, I told him, "Your father's home for a month. But don't you worry about him. We'll just go along, you and me, like we've been doing, and the month will fly by, you'll see, before you even know it."

Barry clutched his sheep and said, "Yahh," which I took to mean, Fine with me.

That same night, I woke up at 3:00 A.M. with a cramped, hollow sensation—and discovered I was getting my very first period. Well, good, I thought, listening to police sirens far away somewhere on the street. This means I'm growing up, getting older. I liked that feeling a lot.

At meals I purposely talked only to Barry so that Robert couldn't distract him from learning how to eat. But that didn't stop Robert from interfering occasionally.

"Your mother's told me all about your work with Barry," Robert said at dinner one night. "Not to mention that I can see it for myself."

I stiffened at that—his watching me. "Hold your spoon, Barry," I said, keeping my voice cheerful and affectionate. "Try to move the spoon with your fingers—like this, see?"

"I think you're just wonderful," Robert said.

"Barry is the wonderful one. He's doing all the work." I wasn't trying to get praise from Robert. "Barry, what a good boy you are! Moving your spoon all by yourself! You deserve a big kiss."

Which was the end of just about the longest conversation Robert and I had that month.

We visited Grandmother Anne and Grandfather Mitchell one Saturday while Robert was home. Mostly I kept Barry away from Grandmother Anne. Soon after we got there, I took Barry to a small lounge in the lobby, and bought him chicken broth from a coffee machine. It was so hot I had to blow and blow on it. Several old ladies smiled and winked at us. One of them wanted to hold Barry, but I had to say no. How could I be sure she'd even listen to me if I tried to explain the right way to do it?

Barry's teachers at UCP gave Loretta a half dozen toy catalogs, and Loretta passed them on to me. "See if there's anything here you think Barry would like," she told me.

The catalogs all had names like, "Toys for the Special Child," and "Let's Play with Our Very Special Children." *Special* didn't mean special in the usual sense—it meant handicapped. Flipping through the catalogs, I remembered a book Robert gave me when I was little, called *A Special Family*. It was all about how it felt to have a father in the navy. "We are a special family," the book said, "because we have to try harder to let each other know we really care about one another."

But now we'd turned into a *special* "special family."

I ordered Play-Doh, Nerf balls, finger paints, magnets, hand puppets, soft blocks, and Chunkies—very easy jigsaw puzzles with extralarge, extrathick pieces. Soon the big blue space in the living room didn't look so empty, not with all these toys.

"What goes where?" I asked Barry, as we sat and stared down at a zoo Chunky. "Let's try again," I said, when he picked up the wrong piece or pointed to the wrong place, which happened nearly always. "See, now the hippopotamus has ears!"

The day Robert left for Connecticut, I brought Barry into my room and changed his diaper on my bed. "See, what did I tell you?" I said. "The whole month went by like it was no time at all. And your father's next shore leave will be just the same."

Barry smiled up at his turtle.

9

Loretta came into my room one night as I was doing my algebra homework. I was sitting at my desk, scribbling away with a number-two pencil, multiplying whole bunches of negative numbers. The air was fresh and cool on this early evening in April, and Barry was taking a nap.

"Promise me something," Loretta said firmly.

I put the pencil down and shoved the papers away. "I'm open to that, if I know what it is," I said.

"Ellen, you've got to promise not to throw her out."

"Throw her out? *Who?* Is Rainbow coming back?"

Loretta placed her hands on her hips, and exhaled deeply. "I've hired a therapist for Barry," she said.

I stared at her. I couldn't believe she hadn't talked to me about this first. "Tell me all about Barry's therapist," I said coolly.

"She's a trained professional with over ten years' experience. Barry's teachers have told me that she's wonderful, and exactly what Barry needs right now. She'll come here every day, Monday through Friday, from four o'clock to six o'clock. And I won't be here, Ellen, I'll be at the library. *You'll* be here."

Two hours, five days a week. It sure cut into my time with Barry. On the other hand . . .

"Barry's teachers said Barry really needs this, right?" I asked, and Loretta nodded. "And she absolutely knows what she's doing?" Loretta nodded again. "All right," I said. "But I want to watch. I want to see every single thing she's doing with Barry."

Loretta looked over at the turtle, who was sticking his head below the water level, and opening his eyes. "I suppose that's all right," she said, "if you don't get in the way, or waste her time with a lot of silly questions."

"I won't waste her time," I said.

"And you won't throw her out," Loretta said.

So I had to promise.

Barry's therapist arrived promptly at four o'clock the next afternoon. She smelled very fresh and clean, and her skin had a well-scrubbed, ruddy look to it. Horn-rimmed glasses circled large brown eyes; she looked about forty, but her hair was already completely gray, parted in the middle and curling around her ears. She wore a white blouse, tan cardigan sweater, brown tweed pants, sensible walking shoes with laces, and a wedding ring. "Are you Ellen Gray, the child's sister?" were her first words to me. Her voice was calm and soft and high-pitched, but something told me she could let out a holler if she wanted to.

"I'm Barry's sister," I announced, wishing I wasn't wearing jeans and a polo shirt, but something older, more serious. A three-piece suit, maybe.

"I am Claire Withers Stonehill," she said, extending a

smooth hand with long, straight fingers like columns. No polish on the short, rounded fingernails. She shook my hand slowly and deliberately, as if every one of her actions, even the most ordinary, required careful thought. "Where is the child?" she asked.

"The child—I mean, Barry, is taking a nap. I'll go and get him."

I brought her back a very groggy Barry in blue over-alls. Tilting her head back, she scrutinized Barry beneath her glasses the way I imagined a jeweler studied an uncut diamond. What have we here? she seemed to be thinking. What can we make out of this?

She reached for Barry and took him gently in her arms; Barry woke up fully with a start, but relaxed right away. Then she knelt down and sat on the carpet, placing Barry in front of her, and began touching his arms and legs.

I sat down on the couch.

Without looking over at me, Claire said, "Are you planning to . . . observe?" She thought about her words too.

"Of course," I said. And thought about my words. "If that's all right with you," I added.

"I am of absolutely no concern," Claire Withers Stonehill replied. "I don't matter one bit. However, if the child is distracted by you, you will have to leave."

"But I can't leave!" I burst out, and then tried to soften it. "Barry's so used to me," I said calmly, trying to match her tone. "It will be much more distracting for him if I'm not here."

"Mmm, we'll see," Claire said, and began to work.

Loretta was right—she was wonderful. Her hands appeared both strong and gentle, as she applied pressure to Barry's right leg. I bet her hands would have performed magic, no matter what she had them doing—painting, sculpting, baking, playing a grand piano. "His right leg has a tendency to curl inward," she said, in a soothing voice that I could see Barry liked. "Let's see if we can straighten out that leg."

After a while, she stood Barry up, placed his hands at his sides, and let go. He stood rigidly for a moment, eyes wide and arms stiff, before swaying into her arms. "He's frightened of falling," she said, rubbing Barry's back. "All children are—it's a natural fear. But Barry will be falling his entire life, and he's got to learn how to do it right."

"What do you mean, do it right?"

"Imagine yourself starting to fall," Claire said. "Instinctively, your arms thrust out in front of your body, or form an X in front of your face. That way you shield your body and face, and break the fall with your arms. Children with cerebral palsy begin to fall—and they fall right smack on their faces. Sitting up one moment, and a bruised forehead or bloody nose in the next."

"But why?" I asked. "Why do they do that?"

And Claire explained it. "Hold up your left hand," she said to me, and I did. "How were you able to do that?"

I shrugged. "I just did it. You told me to."

"To be more accurate, your brain told you to. Every time you move a muscle, from a blink to a fancy dive into a swimming pool, it's because messages are getting sent from your brain to your muscles, very fast and efficient messages. Move this, lift that. And it happens. Do you follow?"

"Yes," I answered.

"Barry has cerebral palsy. 'Cerebral' means brain and 'palsy' means muscles. The part of Barry's brain that sends messages to his muscles was damaged. So his brain is sending out perfectly sensible messages, but sometimes the muscles receive these messages all jumbled and wrong.

You must have played telephone as a child. It's very similar. So you see, when Barry starts to fall, his brain tells his arms to shield his face and body. But his arms might not move at all, or they might tense up, or they might even move backward in the entirely wrong direction."

"But that's awful!" I said.

"It's not wonderful," Claire said reasonably. "Don't you see, that's what therapy is all about. Getting the undamaged parts of Barry's brain to perform for the damaged parts."

"So you think Barry will learn how to fall," I said. "And then he'll walk."

"Time will tell. Barry is unique. Of the seven hundred thousand people in this country with cerebral palsy, no two are exactly alike. Though of course there are similarities within each type. Barry has ataxia. That tells us that Barry will probably always have poor balance, and his speech will probably always be very difficult to understand, and he'll probably need diapers long after children far younger than he is have stopped wearing them, and he'll start to snore, if he hasn't already—"

"He has," I said. Barry, ten years from now, bumping into everything, speaking in garbled sounds, wearing a diaper.

Claire glanced over at me. "Don't look so stricken," she said. "Barry's cerebral palsy is really rather mild, considering. Some children with CP can't move at all. Some children see different images out of each eye, so they can never get a clear picture of the world. Some have very sensitive hearing, so that a whisper sounds like a shout. Some have seizures where they shake all over and stop breathing. Some hallucinate—tasting, seeing, hearing, and smelling things that aren't there. Some have severe mental retardation. Barry may not have any retardation at all, or perhaps

141

only a mild case." She gave Barry a brief hug. "He's a very good child, I can see that. He's trying. He likes to work hard. You see, Ellen, handicapped children are children first; the handicap is second. Barry wants what all children want. To feel loved, and to feel capable."

In my head, I was telling Loretta, "Claire Withers Stonehill is brilliant. She truly understands and appreciates Barry."

When the session was over, Claire stood up, swept a little blue carpet fluff off her pants, and handed Barry back to me.

Suddenly I was bursting with questions about her. "Where do you live?" I asked. "Where'd you go to school? How'd you get interested in becoming a therapist?"

Claire's shoulders tensed up. "All of that," she said crisply, "is irrelevant. What is important here is the child. I am of absolutely no concern whatsoever."

I blinked at her. She sure had a funny way of talking about herself. "I'm sorry," I said.

I saw her shoulders relax. She almost smiled. "It's actually very dull," she said. "My life. Me."

This only made me even more curious about Claire Withers Stonehill.

Claire was never late and never ill; no family emergencies ever called her away. Every weekday, from four o'clock to six o'clock, she was there for Barry with her no-nonsense dedication that I admired more and more with each session. And I was there too, sitting and watching and soaking it all in.

I must have seen Barry start to fall a thousand times, and each time my body flinched, wanting to catch him. Little by little, Barry began to move his arms out in front of him, just before Claire caught him and said, "Very good, Barry. Next time you'll do even better."

Claire showed Barry large, colorful pictures of animals, and tried to get him to speak. "Owl," she said, pointing to a big barn owl with dark eyes and a white, heart-shaped face. "Ow, ow, ow, ow, ow."

After about a million repetitions over several weeks, Barry finally said "ow." Also "zzz," like a bee, and "caw, caw," like a crow. By the end of May, Barry said his very first word while looking at a picture of a turtle in a pond.

"Nellie," he said.

Claire pointed to me. "But that's you!" she cried. "Barry just said your name! He must be thinking about that turtle you bought him. You must be very proud."

Proud? I was definitely confused. "My name is Ellen," I said, as if she didn't know.

"Children with CP often get names backward or mixed-up. I think you'd better get used to Barry calling you 'Nellie.'"

"Okay," I said. It made me think of "The Cow Kicked Nellie in the Belly in the Barn"—but if Barry wanted to call me Nellie, fine with me. "Will he start learning lots of words now?" I asked.

"It's hard to tell. Sometimes there's a little burst of learning, followed by quite a long time when nothing much happens, or the child forgets what he's learned, and you're back to square one. Don't let it worry you. Barry will learn, and keep on learning, because he wants to. All children do. It's just that Barry might not do so at a steady pace."

"Nellie," Barry said, still looking at the turtle.

"That's me," I told Barry. "I'm right here."

One afternoon Claire loaned me a book, called *The Man Who Mistook His Wife for a Hat*, by a doctor named Oliver Sacks. "Read the essay called 'The Disembodied Lady,'" Claire told me, "if you want to know a little more about how Barry might be feeling."

The essay was sort of technical and hard to follow, but I got the general idea. A lady named Christina somehow developed a very mysterious condition. After twenty-seven years of feeling absolutely normal, she suddenly felt as if her hands "wandered," and when she reached for an object, her hand missed the object by a mile. "I can't feel my body," Christina said. "I 'lose' my arms. I think they're one place but I find they're another." She said her body felt blind and deaf to itself. Only when she felt wind on her arms and face did she feel she actually had arms and a face. "It's not the real thing," Christina said, "but it lifts this horrible, dead veil for a while."

It was what we were all trying to do for Barry—lift this horrible, dead veil.

In early June, the air was so damp and sultry that even while taking a cold shower I still felt like I was sweating. But Claire, even on these amazingly hot days, always wore crisp-looking long-sleeved blouses, long cotton pants, and shoes with socks, never sandals.

One day, at the end of her session, Claire didn't get up right away, and dust herself off, and leave promptly. This time she sat quietly for several minutes, and then said to me, "A month ago, your mother mentioned that you might be missing some afternoons."

"What?" I said. "Never! Why would she say that?"

"You might be playing softball, she told me."

I had to laugh. "The tryouts were back in April, and games started up in May, and I deliberately didn't go to any of it. Play softball, instead of this? No way."

Claire smiled faintly. "You remind me of myself," she said.

Well, I nearly fell off the couch. This was quite a personal remark, coming from someone who absolutely refused to talk about herself. "Thank you," I said, feeling complimented. Why did I feel a little scared too?

"You're serious about Barry," Claire said, more or less as a question.

"Absolutely," I replied.

"Some children—they say they want to learn about caring for their handicapped siblings, but after a day or two they're back to playing with their friends."

"I'm here," I said, "because it's exactly where I want to be."

Claire leaned back on her palms. I noticed her long, taut neck. "I have an older sister named Jillie," she said. "She has Down's syndrome. I thought you might like to hear about her."

"Yes," I said, stunned. It had also happened with Maribeth—finding out that other people had this in their families too. I leaned back into the couch, trying to match Claire's casualness. "Down's syndrome," I said. "Is that like what Barry has?"

"No. Barry has brain damage. Down's syndrome is a chromosome defect. Jillie's nose is flat, and her eyes are slanted—she looks almost Asian, which is why Down's used to be called mongolism, because people with Down's looked as though they were from Mongolia. Jillie has mental

145

retardation. When I was a child, I didn't know anything about chromosomes, of course, and I thought Jillie was the way she was because she'd been hit by lightning. Isn't that silly? But to this day I'm frightened of thunderstorms."

I felt that for as long we sat here, I could ask her anything and actually get some answers. It was as if a hole in the universe was opening up to another dimension. "Does Jillie live with you and your husband?" I asked. I knew she was married, from the wedding ring.

"No. Richard and I live in Stuyvesant Town at Fourteenth Street. He's a junior high school English teacher." Claire took a deep breath, and then spoke in a sort of detached way, the way doctors do sometimes. "Jillie lives in a group home in Queens, not far from my parents. It's the best place for Jillie. She shares the home with seven other adults, all with Down's. Three nurses attend to them, but Jillie is expected to keep her own room clean, and cook dinner twice a week. Jillie has a full-time job. She works in a hospital kitchen—she prepares salads. On her vacations, she travels all over the country, and abroad. With supervision, of course."

"That's wonderful," I said. "You must have really helped Jillie a lot."

Claire took off her glasses and rubbed her eyes. "I was the younger one," she said. "No, it was my parents. They believed in Jillie from the very beginning, at a time when most people thought a child like Jillie should be shipped off to an institution before she destroyed the entire family. From the very beginning, my parents decided that Jillie was going to live the fullest possible life. Down's children are often overweight, but my parents fed her lots of fresh fruits and raw vegetables, and to this day Jillie is slender and athletic. My mother taught her to wash and keep herself clean. Jillie's had clarinet lessons. The only thing she couldn't learn about was money. She thinks two bills are always worth more than one, even when the two bills are one dollar each, and the single bill is a ton."

"Does Jillie have a boyfriend?" I wasn't exactly sure why I asked that. Maybe because she seemed to have everything else.

Claire paused, put her glasses back on, frowned at me. I could see her trying to decide if I was old enough to hear this. I guess she figured, yes. "Sexuality cannot be part of Jillie's life," she said. "My mother had to teach her that nobody but Mother, Sister, or Doctor may see her underpants. Even so, there was . . . an episode. A man who lived near the home had gotten Jillie's clothes off and had taken her picture."

I drew in my breath. Who would do that?

"Luckily, she didn't get pregnant. She couldn't possibly care for a child, and there's a chance the child might have had Down's too." Claire's voice took on an edge. I guess she'd had to think about all of this a little too often.

"Do you visit Jillie a lot?" I asked.

"I visit Jillie," Claire said—leaving off the "a lot."

"Were you close, as children?"

Claire paused even longer and frowned even more severely. This part seemed to be even more personal than Jillie's sexuality. "I can see that you want to know. I can see how serious you are about Barry. And I also see that you're maturing far more quickly than your peers. Well. I was angry all the time." Claire stated it as a fact. "Angry at Jillie, and at my parents, and at God, though not necessarily in that order." She smiled a little to herself. "I didn't know it then, of course. Everybody adored Jillie. I adored her too. Or should I say I was told that I adored her. Ordered to do so."

I could feel it—Claire's anger, as if it were charging the air with static electricity.

"When I was in eighth grade, my team won the debating contest for the entire district. We were supposed to go to Albany for the state championship, and all our teachers said we were sure to win it. I had this talent for debating, you see. Rebuttal was my specialty. I could organize my thoughts instantly and express them concisely. And it was what I wanted more than anything, to be a state debating champion." Her voice dropped. "But the day of the championship, Jillie got sick, and I had to stay home with her. My mother was not about to take the day off from work, and it never occurred to her to ask a neighbor or relative to help out. It was simply assumed that this was my duty in life. My team went up to Albany and were eliminated immediately. I cried for days. Why did Jillie get sick—to spite me, because she could never be a state debating champion? Why did my mother force me to stay home? Why did God let everything happen as it did? I felt sinful too, because I cared more about the debating championship than about Jillie."

"Was she very sick?"

"Hardly at all. She had an earache, and an outbreak of eczema, which she gets when she's stressed. The doctor drained her ears, and that night she was as perky as ever. The eczema disappeared by itself."

There was silence for a little while. "You were right," I said slowly. "You were right to be angry."

Claire smiled. "I know that now. I know many things now. That my mother was wrong to take Jillie's side when

I said that she threw her lunch box at me. 'It's not in Jillie's nature,' my mother insisted. What did that make me, then—a liar? In the middle of the night, Jillie slapped me as I slept. My mother said I must have provoked her. While sleeping? I was expected to be a perfect student, and even a report card with four As and one B was criticized. When I was in high school, Jillie decided to 'color' one of my book reports, covering it with red and orange smudges. I . . . had a kind of breakdown, is the only way to describe it. I screamed and screamed at my parents. At the same time I could sort of stand outside myself and watch myself screaming. It was horrible. I said that my life had been sacrificed for Jillie's. I said I wanted to leave home and never, ever come back." Claire's neck flushed a deep red.

"What happened?" I said.

Claire shrugged. "My parents cried. I cried. Jillie cried. The whole world cried, but nothing changed. My mother thought I was jealous of Jillie, and wasn't that ridiculous— a girl endowed with a normal mind and body. 'Thank God you're healthy,' my mother always said, though it sounded more like a curse than a blessing. My parents didn't understand. They never understood. They never even tried."

Claire's parents may have worked miracles with Jillie— but look what had happened to Claire. Huge parts of Claire had been left behind.

You remind me of myself, Claire had said.

The hole in the universe closed up.

10

My clothes weren't acting right.

Last summer's tank tops pinched the skin under my arms, and barely covered my chest; I couldn't get the shorts up past my hips. I imagined weird moths that attacked only during the winter and, instead of chewing up wool sweaters, shrank cotton clothes down a size or two. It was that, or I'd grown an entirely new body. But when I looked in the mirror, all I could see was the same old Ellen Gray.

One Saturday afternoon, Loretta suggested we go shopping, but I told her I didn't want to waste money like that, not when Barry outgrew his clothes every few months.

"What about your birthday money from Robert?" Loretta asked. "We can buy some T-shirts at the Gap." She groaned when I told her I'd given it to Rainbow. "She was here for six minutes and you paid her for six hours!"

"Why can't I borrow some of your stuff?" I said. "I like that light green shift of yours. And your khaki shorts, and that sleeveless white top . . ."

Loretta frowned at me. "You're sure you want to wear my clothes?"

"Why not?" I said. "There's nothing wrong with that, is there?"

She seemed to be thinking hard. "I don't know. Maybe. No, I suppose not."

So I began to wear Loretta's clothes.

Eighth-grade graduation meant another special assembly. I sat in the auditorium, wearing Loretta's short-sleeved, scoop-necked, lavender rayon dress and her taupe pumps—even her shoes fit me—with my hair piled up on top of my head, because of the heat. A whole bunch of people, including Susie Brockleman and Ms. Stapler, told me I was looking "so grown-up." They all looked surprised when I said thank you.

School was over! And I was looking forward to spending even more time with Barry. Wheeling him around the streets of Soho on soft summer nights; playing in the sandbox in Washington Square Park; showing him trees and cars and dogs, and trying to get him to say the words.

But all that changed with a phone call.

I was feeding Barry some spaghetti for dinner, the night before Robert came home again. The phone rang; Loretta went to answer it, and came back all excited. "Wonderful news!" she said. "That was Robert in Scotland. He says he'll be home all summer!"

"Wait a minute," I said, wiping my hands on a napkin that was already soaked with spaghetti sauce. "Wait. Daddy's coming home in July, I know that. But in August he'll be going up to Connecticut."

"That's the wonderful news. He got permission to spend almost all of August at home with us, and still take his next patrol in September, as planned. He's cut through a lot of red tape to arrange this, El."

I shook my head and went back to feeding Barry.

"Now I can work full-time at the library this summer," Loretta went on cheerfully.

"But you can't," I said, hearing myself whine. "Who'll go to UCP with Barry?"

She was all dimples. "Robert. He's so eager to get started. He wants to take over every aspect of Barry's care this summer, and sit in on the sessions with Claire—you know, the way you do."

"But he can't," I said, trying hard not to whine anymore. "He doesn't know what he's doing. He's not the one who's been studying Claire for three months!"

"He'll learn, El. Just the way you have." Then she added the kicker: "And you can help him."

And did he ever need me!

As soon as Robert came home, he started in immediately: "Ellen, am I feeding Barry correctly?" And washing him the right way, and doing this exercise properly, and carrying him the way he's supposed to be carried?

"Let Barry hold his spoon by himself," I told Robert at dinner. "Don't use Loretta's shampoo," I said at bath time. "Use the gentle one, see? The one for babies." As Robert changed Barry's diaper, I said, "Make sure Barry pushes his leg into your hand, hard." And throughout the evening, I told him, "Don't carry him so much. Let Barry crawl around by himself."

"You sound so critical," Loretta told me after Robert had been home for a few days.

"It's my way of helping," I reminded her. "Besides, when it comes to Barry, everything must be done exactly right."

152

*　*　*

I could see Robert enjoying himself no end, telling us at dinner everything he'd learned at UCP that day. But the summer was moving very slowly for me. Every morning I slept late, and then took a walk with no destination, though sometimes I ended up at an art gallery or a movie. Always, I got home in time for Claire, but the time with Claire wasn't the same, now that Robert was sitting beside me on the couch.

In late July, Claire tried something new with Barry. She held a small Hula Hoop around his waist, and told him to grip the sides. Then she slowly pulled the Hula Hoop forward, saying, "Now let's see you take a few steps."

Barry looked over at Robert, and then placed one foot in front of the other, very shaky and awkward.

"He's walking on the insides of his feet," Claire said. "That's why he's so wobbly."

"But he's walking!" Robert said breathlessly.

As if Barry's first steps were just for him.

By August, Robert had grown so confident with Barry that he hardly ever asked me questions anymore. But I stayed close by, and kept an eagle eye on everything he did, just in case. Even after he started calling me "Shadow"!

"I helped Barry use a walker today," Robert told us at dinner one night. "Loretta, we'll have to buy a walker for Barry to use at home."

"What do you mean, a walker?" I asked. My lap was feeling so empty without Barry. "You mean, like what old people use to get around?"

"Exactly right, Shadow," Robert said. "Only much smaller, of course. And with wheels and handlebars. Barry did exceptionally well on it, his teacher said."

Barry, with a spoon in his mouth, stared up at Robert, fascinated.

"Look, he's biting the spoon!" I said. "You have to watch him very carefully! Tell him to close his lips around the spoon!"

"Oh, yes," Robert said, smiling down at Barry, who smiled right back. "Barry, close your lips, like this . . . yes, that's right."

Did Loretta see trouble ahead? Did Robert care that a tiny child was growing more attached by the hour to an occasional visitor from under the oceans? No to both questions. All Loretta seemed to talk about was how great it was that the "family of four" was together again. And Robert continued to lavish his attention on Barry every waking moment, right up through his last night home in late August, when he put Barry to bed for the last time.

"This is Barry's mouth," Robert was telling him, touching his lips, as I stood there and observed. "Barry can talk out of his mouth. He can say words, like *Nellie* and *Daddy*."

Yes—Barry could say *Daddy* now.

Robert turned to me and frowned. "Shadow, I feel like I've forgotten something," he said. "Have I forgotten anything?"

The words came out of me before I could stop them: "You forgot to tell him he's doing great, and that you love him so much, and that you'll never leave him, not ever."

Robert just stared at me. "Ellen, I can't promise that. You know I can't."

I knew.

That last week in August, Claire took off for vacation—and I had Barry all to myself, except for his time at UCP.

"We'll have the best week!" I told Barry the first morning

154

at breakfast as he sat on my lap. "When you get home from school, we'll go to the park and play in the sandbox. Barry, I'm so happy to have you back. I missed you like crazy."

"Daddy," Barry said, trying to look behind me.

I took a deep breath. "No, it's Nellie," I said. "Nellie's here with you."

"Daddy," Barry said again.

I hugged him, hard. "Barry, it's Nellie. Nellie's got you now."

In the afternoon, I folded up the walker and attached it to the back of Barry's stroller, the way people hook their own small shopping carts onto the large ones in a supermarket. "Look, Barry, there's a policeman on a horse," I told him, as we traveled uptown. "See, when the light is green, we can cross the street. Can you say 'go' and 'green?' "

"Grrr," Barry growled.

Every few blocks, I took Barry out of the stroller, and let him practice his wobble-walk with the walker. "Just a few steps," I said. "Keep your balance now."

Most people just passed us by, with barely a glance in our direction. But what amazed me was how some people on the street stared at Barry . . . and stared . . . and *stared*. What's wrong with that child? I could see in their eyes. Who's with him? Is there something wrong with her too?

On the other side of Houston Street, two women in wide-brimmed straw hats passed by, and I heard one tell the other, "God has punished her by giving her a child like that."

Oh, wow, I thought. She thinks I'm Barry's mother! It took a moment for the cruelty of her statement to sink in.

Barry took a few steps inside Washington Square Park,

155

stumbled, and landed on his knees. A boy circled us on his skateboard, whizzing by in a blur of orange clothing. "Hey, kid, have a nice trip, see you next fall!" he called out, laughing, and then he was gone.

I picked Barry up. He wasn't hurt. I wanted to trip that boy and give him a fall. My anger . . . it felt like moss all over my skin. It scared me a little.

I sat next to Barry inside a big oval sandbox. We pretended to "wash our hands" in the sand, an exercise Claire had told me about. It was supposed to teach Barry how to—guess what? Wash his hands. We were surrounded by a bunch of kids playing with pails and shovels, as parents and baby-sitters watched from nearby benches.

Barry loved the sand, so soft and loose in his fingers. He started to laugh, and then let out some garbled, thick, nasal sounds that weren't exactly words yet.

Almost immediately, a woman with dark frizzy hair rushed over from bench and yanked up a boy in a red baseball cap by his wrist. "Don't sit near that child!" she said. "How do we know why he's like that?"

"He's not contagious," I explained, but the woman was already halfway out of the park, dragging off her son in a long, sweeping stride while his legs pumped to keep up.

Barry stopped playing and sat there quietly for a moment.

"Let's play some more," I told him. "Show me how you can hold a clump of sand, and then let it go."

A few minutes later, a girl with soft blond curls and chocolate smeared on her lips walked across the sand to Barry. "My daddy says your hands are capped," she said proudly. She was about five years old.

"What?" I said. "Oh, you mean *handicapped*. Yes, that's right, he has cerebral palsy. And I know he'd like to meet you. His name is Barry."

"I'm Melissa," she said, even more proudly. "You have to talk for him?"

"He's not ready to talk yet," I said, and explained a little bit about cerebral palsy.

"Will he die?" Melissa asked. I said no. "Will he get all better?" I said no again. Melissa scrunched up her face. "But that's sad," she said.

Just then a soft male voice said, "Melissa." I looked up to see Melissa's father. He had hair everywhere you never wanted to see it on the human body—back of the hands, shoulders, neck. "That boy might be very upset that he's that way," he told Melissa carefully. "Maybe he had a terrible accident and doesn't want to remember it."

"No, he's—," I began. Suddenly I felt very tired. "Byebye," I told Melissa, and she waved before grabbing her father's hairy hand.

Barry stared down into the sand, frowning. I couldn't get him to play anymore. "There'll be better days," I told him. A little while later, he poked me in the arm. He was ready to go home now. So was I.

The next day was so hot I could actually see the heat—thick, slow, wavy, shimmering. We didn't go very far that day. A few blocks from the loft, while Barry was practicing with the walker, I saw Susie Brockleman emerge from the heat as though she were a mirage. But no such luck—she was real.

"What," she said, drawing back, her brown eyes opening wide, "is *that*?"

"That," I responded, "is my brother, Barry."

"I meant, why's he holding on to that thing?"

"He's got cerebral palsy," I said, and explained it—blah, blah, blah.

157

"Oh," Susie said, without a hint of understanding.

A man walking two Labrador retrievers swept by us, and Barry called out, "Nellie! Gorrgg, Cee-Cee!"

"No, Barry, that's not George and Gracie," I said. "But they sure do look a lot like George and Gracie."

Susie bit her lip, and then asked, "Does he talk that way because he wants to, or because he has to?"

I sighed. "He's trying to talk, same as you and me. His therapist says he's doing very well."

"He has a therapist?" Susie squinted at me. "My mom goes to one 'cause she grinds her teeth. You mean like that?"

Clearly kids my own age were dumb. Why was it taking them so long to grow up? I explained it some more, but Susie's pretty face just pouted at me.

"I feel so bad for him," she said.

"Don't," I told her firmly. "He's a kid, a regular kid, and he wants you to like him, or hate him, or not care about him at all—anything but pity him."

"Can't help it," Susie said, as sadly as if Barry had died long ago. But Barry was standing right there in front of her, and he had his whole life ahead of him.

I wasn't too sorry when for the next few days New York City got hit by long, rumbling thunderstorms with record rainfall.

On our last day out, I left the walker home and took Barry in his stroller to a festival in Little Italy—whole streets closed off to traffic, full of rides, and stands selling spicy sausage heros, and pastries stuffed full of creamy custard, and games where you can throw darts and win enormous stuffed animals. I had a sausage hero—it was incredibly good—and let Barry eat all the cream inside a pastry.

We passed something called a Tilt-A-Whirl, a ride with teacup-shaped seats that spun wildly all around.

"Nellie, Nellie!" Barry said, pointing at the ride.

But I wasn't sure it was right for Barry. Claire had once told me that a child with CP should never be thrown in the air, or experience any sudden, drastic changes in movement. "It's utterly confusing for them," Claire explained, and compared it to getting caught by a wave in the ocean.

"No," I told him.

Barry kept begging. He wouldn't stop.

Finally I gave in. The man who sold me two tickets said he would keep an eye on Barry's stroller.

And Barry was fine! He loved it! The teacup tilted up, spun slowly to the left, and then very fast to the right. Then we tilted down and started the whole thing all over again. Afterward, my ears pounded, and I knew my face was pea green, and it was a miracle I didn't throw up. Even so, I had to sit down on a curb and fold my arms around my head.

"Nellie, Nellie!" Barry begged again.

"No," I said flatly, into my knees. "And this time no means no."

I looked up a minute later—and Barry was gone. I spun around as wildly as our teacup. Where was Barry? Panic filled my throat.

But there was Barry, only a few feet away, hugging a young woman who was kneeling down, hugging him back.

She had light brown eyes and two thick blond braids like ropes. "Who is he?" she asked me, softly. "He sort of stumbled over to me, and said something I couldn't understand. I leaned down to hear him better, and he threw his arms around my neck. It was the best hug I ever got!"

"Barry, you scared me," I said. "You really scared me."

"I'm sure he didn't mean to," the young woman said. "His name is Barry? What was Barry trying to tell me?"

"He probably wanted you to take him on the Tilt-A-Whirl again," I said.

She laughed. "I hate that ride," she said. "But I could use some more of those hugs." And she gave him three more rides.

"See, Barry," I said on our way home, "I told you there'd be better days."

Geometry was my first class on my first day of ninth grade. From the door of the classroom, I spotted the chair I wanted—front row, way over by the windows. It was close enough to see the board and ask questions, but not surrounded by a lot of other kids. Strange, the classroom looked different this year. Someone had lowered the ceiling and shortened all the furniture.

As I circled around the teacher's desk, I heard somebody behind me ask, "Excuse me, miss? Are you subbing for this class?" I turned around and looked down at the fuzzy brown hair of a woman in a houndstooth suit, carrying an armload of papers. What was she talking about? I wondered. How could I see the top of her head? Was she that short—or had I grown so much taller? "The front office sent me," she chatted away, brown eyes darting all around as she spoke. "I'm sure it's a mistake—first day chaos, the usual. Shall I go back and tell the front office that they sent two substitute teachers for the same class?"

I just stood there, and saw myself in her eyes—tall, in a blue pleated skirt, crisp off-white blouse, shiny blue pumps, hair neatly pulled back in a clip, and carrying a leather attaché case with a zipper all around it. I glanced across the room at thirty kids trying hard not to laugh and give me away and knew that if I claimed to be the substitute teacher, I'd be popular instantly. My neck felt all tingly. It would be such a nervy thing to do!

But then I remembered shoplifting, and getting caught, and crying in the dim room at Paper Moon. If I had fun now, I might be kept after school, and that would be so unfair to Barry.

"It's your class," I told the woman. "I'm a student."

She flushed and put a hand to her mouth, and the whole class groaned in disappointment. "Well, take your seat, then," she told me sternly, as if I'd purposely played a trick on her. I took my seat, the one in the front row by the window. "Let x equal twelve," she began, reviewing the algebra that everybody had forgotten over the summer.

Let $x = 12$ . . . . Let them all be disappointed in me, I was thinking. Not one of them knew what it felt like to have Barry for a brother—absolutely proud of it, and absolutely alone.

I stayed in the cafeteria all through lunch period, even though it was bright and cool outside. I didn't want to get Loretta's clothes all dirty. That meant almost fifty minutes in a wooden chair that curved in exactly the wrong way for the human rear end, pulled up to a Formica-top table that was sticky even before I got there. Lunch that day was a stew that had nothing recognizable in it—it was pink cubes, whitish blocks, and a yellow gravy. I was thinking about Barry as I pushed the stew around the plate. Daddy, Daddy, he'd started saying again, all through breakfast. No, Barry, it's Nellie. Nellie's here.

Somebody sat down next to me. Ray Frost. The guy I

used to cheat off of. The guy Faye and Muriel had called "a drip," and "a big nothing," and not as cute as his identical twin brother, Bob. Both brothers had short, light blond hair, and green eyes that were a little too close together, and freckles all over. Probably Bob was cuter. Ray's skin was paler, so the freckles stood out more, and the sun this summer had nearly bleached his hair; he looked like a sunstreaked photograph. Also, he smelled of English Leather.

"I'm in your geometry class," he said, opening up a halfpint of milk. "I couldn't understand how that sub thought you were another teacher. You don't look old or anything—you just look very mature."

"I know I'm a party pooper," I said. "You don't have to tell me."

"Oh, no!" Ray said. "I understand why you did what you did. They'd have had your head for that." And he smiled a big, warm, terrific, freckled smile at me.

I wanted to hug him. I nearly hugged him. Barry would have. I imagined Ray calling me and asking me out, and going out with him, and again, and again, my head filling up with this guy, leaving no room for Barry, who needed me, who'd miss me . . . and why? Just so I could have a boyfriend.

"Speaking of geometry," I said coolly, "I've got to do my homework."

"Want to do it together?"

"Sorry, I can't work that way. I can only think inside my own head." Boy, did that sound dumb.

"You haven't tried thinking with me," Ray said—and there was that smile again. "You might end up twice as smart."

"Or twice as sorry," I said, and stared down into my stew.

162

CHAPTER

11

He wasn't my Barry anymore. It happened on a Wednesday in the last week of September. Barry woke up and began to cry. And wouldn't stop. I changed his diaper, and got him dressed for school, and still Barry wouldn't stop.

At breakfast, Barry shook his head at the sight of a spoonful of oatmeal.

"Won't you eat, for Nellie?" I asked him.

"Daddy," he wailed, and I stuck the food in his open mouth. But he just spit it right back out.

"Let me try something," Loretta said. She filled up a baby bottle with milk, took Barry in her arms, and tilted his head way back. He lay very still.

"He's too old for that!" I said. "You're treating him like he's a hopeless case."

"Ellen, he's eating," Loretta said.

In the afternoon, I shined the flashlight on Barry's arm, and leg, and belly. I spread out all of his toys and games, placing the pieces in Barry's hands. I let his turtle crawl around on the carpet, and told Barry to crawl after him. But there was no response to any of it, only tears.

"He's crying all the time!" I told Claire at four o'clock. "He won't do anything!"

"I know," Claire said mildly, kneeling down on the floor beside Barry. "Your mother called me from UCP. Well, this happens. Sometimes learning has to take two steps backward before it can take one step forward."

"Daddy," Barry cried, as Claire wrapped her arms around him.

"He's so tense," Claire said. "Barry, shh, you relax now. You take some deep breaths and relax. In, out, in, out."

Claire and Barry just sat there, breathing together.

"Aren't you going to make him do something?" I asked.

"He's doing something right now," Claire replied. "He's being very quiet."

"But he's not learning anything! Come on, you know how to get him going."

Claire put a finger to her lips, telling me to speak more softly. "It won't do any good to push him beyond his present limits," she whispered. "Let this thing run its course."

"So, okay, we'll wait it out. What'll it take, another half hour? No more than forty-five minutes, right?"

After a few more deep breaths with Barry, Claire said, "Ellen, please leave. You're making the child too tense."

"No," I said. "I'm just as relaxing for Barry as you are." And I folded my arms and sat there.

At dinner, Loretta told me to stay away from Claire, at least for a while. "Claire knows exactly what she's doing," Loretta said, as Barry lay in her arms and gulped loudly from a bottle. "Barry's having an especially hard time right now—"

"And why is that?" As if I didn't know who was to blame for all of this.

"He misses his father," Loretta said—with what sounded

a little like pride! "Claire thinks that for the past month Barry's been waiting for Robert to return, and that now Barry is afraid Robert will never come home. This has brought on a temporary regression—a return to infantile behavior. But Barry will learn that Robert's visits form a pattern, and that Robert will always come home, eventually. Barry will adjust, the way we all have. He's becoming a real member of the family."

Oh, brother! Talk about twisting the truth into a pretzel!

I had a test in social studies the next day, something about small villages and big cities. On the very first question, my mind went blank. Okay, I told myself, it'll come back. But it was so silent in my head, all I could hear were pens scratching away at paper, and feet knocking into chairs, and the buzz of the electric clock over the blackboard. I went to the bathroom and splashed cold water on my face. Does this mean I'm going to start moving backward too? I asked the dripping face in the mirror. I'd skipped a grade once. Will I get left back now? Will I end up like Barry? But when I blotted my face with the rough paper towels, I realized I knew exactly how to answer the first question on the test. It was really very simple. I ran back to the classroom and wrote fast, and had only four questions left when the bell rang.

"I'm not here," I told Claire at five o'clock that afternoon. I was on my way from my room to the kitchen for a Coke and some Peek Freans. I barely glanced at Claire and Barry, but couldn't help noticing that all Claire was doing was just sitting there, stroking Barry's hair, whispering to him. And to think Loretta paid her for this!

On Friday I got my social studies test back—an eighty-five. It was my first grade under a ninety since January. I threw it away.

* * *

Saturday morning, the first day of October, and Barry was still crying. That made it four days and counting.

Loretta asked me to prepare a bottle of milk for Barry with a phenobarbital pill in it. An hour after breakfast, Barry fell asleep on the living room couch. "Why's he tired now?" Loretta said. "He never sleeps so early."

That was when I realized what had happened. I saw myself getting the bottle ready. It was like a movie I was watching for the first time: A girl washed a bottle. She put a pill in the bottom of the bottle. She poured milk in the bottle. Then the girl completely forgot the first pill and put in another.

"I made a mistake," I told Loretta. "I gave Barry two pills. It was a mistake."

Loretta's eyes widened. She picked Barry up and went to her room to call Barry's pediatrician. I followed and stood at her door. "So he's not in any danger," Loretta was saying into the phone. "But even so, he may sleep right through until tomorrow morning. He'll wake up hungry. All right, thank you, I understand." She hung up. She turned to face me. "I'll give Barry his medication from now on," she said. I noticed her hands were shaking a little.

"It was only a mistake! Please, give me another chance."

"Not with this."

Loretta put Barry in his crib, and then took off to visit Maribeth. I stood over the crib several times that day, and spoke to Barry as he slept. Maybe I could reach his dreaming mind. "You've got to forget about your father, Barry," I said. "That's what I did. You'll be a lot happier. Look at me, I'm a lot happier."

The sky turned purply as Loretta and I shared a pizza

that night. We didn't talk much, just listened to Barry snore the hours away.

The next morning, Loretta sat in the middle of her bed, surrounded by the pages of the Sunday *New York Times* spread out like the petals of a flower. I was pacing around, waiting for Barry to wake up. All the windows were open, and crisp air filled every room, and outside I heard leaves rustling.

Just before noon, Barry said, "Daddy," and started to cry.

Loretta leaped off her bed and gave Barry a big kiss. "Good morning!" she said.

"Poor Barry, he's still crying." What I really wanted to say to him was, Couldn't you listen to me at all?

"He's so hungry," Loretta said. "That might account for some of these tears. Come on, sweetheart, let's get you something to eat."

We all went to the kitchen, where Loretta prepared a bottle for Barry, and fed him. And all I did was sit there.

"I think his diaper needs changing," I remarked.

Loretta carried Barry off to his crib, with me close behind. "I'll do it," she said.

Whoa. That sounded awfully familiar.

"Aren't you going to do his exercise?" I asked. "You know, the one where he—"

"I know the one. I'll do it when Barry's ready. Ellen, wait for me in the living room, will you? We need to talk."

So I sat on the couch and waited. Sitting around—it was all I was doing lately.

Loretta came in and sat down beside me. "I'm Barry's mother," she told me.

I frowned, crossed my legs, scratched the back of my neck. "We both know that," I said evenly.

"Yes, but I think we've both forgotten it. Ellen, for a long time you were wonderful with Barry. I was so grateful, I didn't see—maybe I didn't want to see—that really you had become too wonderful. Maribeth warned me about it. She said it wasn't right, the big sister doing everything. It was bad for Barry, and bad for me too, and especially for you—"

"Wait a minute," I said. "It was bad for Barry? *I'm* bad for Barry?"

"Honey, you push him a little too hard, you expect a little too much—"

"That's right," I said, my throat tightening. "I love Barry. I love Barry to pieces."

"Of course you do," Loretta said. She tried to hold my hand. I pulled it away. "But you love Barry too fiercely. Maribeth says it looks to her like you're trying to make something up to Barry. The way she put it was, 'Ellen's been helping herself to a double scoop of guilt, with sprinkles.' "

I could picture Maribeth saying it. A double scoop. Guilt for wrecking Barry. And guilt for hating Barry, because I'd wrecked him. "What do the sprinkles mean?" I asked Loretta.

She smiled. "It's just Maribeth's way of talking. She could have said a triple scoop, or a banana split."

But I knew that if Maribeth had meant a banana split, she would have said it.

"El, you've taken on too much, and it's been forcing you to be too grown-up. I never wanted you to grow up in a hurry, and yet I was allowing it to happen, even helping it

168

along. You're still only thirteen! You've got to be a teenager for six more years, before you can be the adult Ellen Gray is supposed to become."

I wondered if Claire Withers Stonehill was the adult she was supposed to have become.

"I'm Barry's mother," Loretta said again. "I'll take care of Barry from now on."

"No!" I went completely rigid. "You can't take Barry away, Mom, you just can't."

"Ellen, this almost has nothing to do with you."

"No! If you take Barry away, what's going to be left of me?"

Loretta smoothed the hair off my forehead. I didn't push her hand away. Her touch seemed to reach inside and soothe my thoughts. "Plenty," she said. "There's plenty left of you. All of you is left."

We sat quietly for a while. The wolf mother in me knew she had to die. She sure didn't want to. But Barry wasn't a real wolf cub, and the wolf mother wasn't a real wolf or a real mother. I was glad it was October, with leaves dying too, turning dazzling, vivid colors and falling to the ground in crunchy piles.

Loretta put me on a strict schedule and wrote it out on a calendar on our kitchen wall. I was allowed to wake up Barry and feed him breakfast on Mondays and Wednesdays (but I couldn't give him his pill); bathe him and put him to bed on Tuesdays and Thursdays (Thursday was the night of Loretta's parents' group). Also I could watch Claire on Fridays and play with Barry Saturday afternoons.

It didn't feel like enough, not nearly enough! Especially during the first week, when Barry snapped back to being his old self. That Tuesday, he woke up smiling, and let Loretta feed him with a spoon, and walked with the walker very fast, if still very wobblingly, for Claire. By Friday, he'd actually learned some new words—*ball, Mommy,* and, for some reason, *pig.* Though the way Barry spoke, they sounded like "buhll," "Bommy," "big."

"How will I fill my time tomorrow?" I asked Loretta Saturday night at dinner. "You won't let me anywhere near Barry on Sundays."

"You can be near me," she said, blotting Barry's chin. "Why not spend the day with me? In fact, why don't we spend every Sunday together? I could put that on the calendar too—Ellen and Loretta's Day."

The idea made me feel warm inside. "But who'll watch Barry?" I said.

"I still have Rainbow's number."

We went to Macy's on our first Sunday. Surrounded by eight mirrors in an octagon-shaped dressing room, I saw what everybody else had been seeing for months. I'd grown taller. My legs were long. I was a little short-waisted, but no question about it, as far as bodies go, this one wasn't too bad. I chose a few skirts, a couple of sweaters, some pants, and bras that were one letter closer to Z than my old ones.

"Finally, you're getting clothes that are right for you, and I can have my own clothes back!" Loretta cheered.

Also, I got a haircut at a place in Greenwich Village. Loretta read magazines while a man snipped away at my head. "Let's feather your hair, yes?" he said. I prayed it wouldn't look like a pillow after a pillow fight. It didn't. It looked very nice—falling lightly on my forehead in bangs that weren't exactly even, and the rest just brushing my shoulders. Loretta swore I looked like Barbara Stanwyck.

So then we rented an old movie called *The Lady Eve*, just so I could see what Barbara Stanwyck looked like.

Loretta was crazy. Barbara Stanwyck was *gorgeous*.

Pretty soon Sundays became the second best day of the week (Saturdays with Barry still ranked first). Loretta and I went to a soda fountain near Central Park and had two malteds apiece; played checkers at a bistro on the Upper East Side; finished off a pound of incredible pistachio nuts from an old-time store in Tribeca; went to the Museum of Modern Art and hardly spoke at all—those were some of my favorite hours, filled with paintings and silence.

On the way home one Sunday, we stopped off at the supermarket we go to across the street. As we stood behind half a dozen people waiting to pay for their groceries, I caught Loretta staring at the couple at the head of the line. The man, tall and pencil-thin, was unloading paper towels from a shopping cart; the woman wore a puffy off-white down coat that made her look wrapped in marshmallow. "It's here somewhere," she was telling the cashier. "My coupon. Forty cents off Bounty."

Several people ahead of us groaned, but Loretta said, "I see couples like that, and I envy them. Just look at those two. They're like something in a fairy tale."

This sounded very weird to me. Whenever I thought of fairy tales, there were never any men with shopping carts or women with coupons. But then I felt it. Loretta's loneliness, like an ache in the back of the throat. I hadn't really ever considered it before. Loretta, losing her parents at seventeen. And losing Robert every few months. And each loss, even the little ones, echoing all the others.

"Mom, I guess it gets very lonely for you, doesn't it?"

Loretta straightened her shoulders. "I manage," she said.

"But it must be terribly hard. You can talk to me about it, if you want. I mean, wake me up, even. Not for a comedian on the 'Tonight Show.' For you."

She looked at me for a moment. "You understand more, don't you, El? It's because of Barry, isn't it? Barry's taught you some things."

I shrugged. "I don't know," I said, not sure whether I'd learned anything or not.

"I can remember, not so long ago—if something was unpleasant or sad, you'd run off and pretend it wasn't happening."

"Run off?" I said. I saw the face of the girl who had played first base on the softball team two years ago. Roz Spinak. She told me her mother died, and basically I barely spoke to her again.

"Aha!" the woman in the marshmallow coat called out, holding up her coupon in triumph. Then the line moved forward.

Barry calmly smiled up at Robert when he saw him next, which was in November. There were no tears, and there was no fuss, and no drama—and that was just fine with me.

I didn't see much of Robert that month, except at dinner, because he was busy all the time, working at the CHINFO office in midtown. CHINFO stands for Chief of Naval Information—when a story about the navy comes up, it's the people at CHINFO who talk to the press.

"The people at CHINFO are thinking of hiring me next November," he told us one night. "If a position materializes, I'll be home during my next shore duty, not up in Connecticut. Home, for two calendar years."

"Robert, that's wonderful!" Loretta cried. "Ellen, you

remember how wonderful it was to have Robert home all that time?"

"Yes," I said. I did remember. "Is it definite?"

Robert said no, and Loretta added, "I'll try not to get my hopes up." She paused, then laughed. "Too late. They're already up."

Loretta and I spent one frosty Sunday afternoon at Maribeth's art gallery in Tribeca. It wasn't for a fancy, dressy opening or anything. I'd still never been there, and I wanted to see it.

Her gallery was called Cave, and the name was a perfect fit. It was small, only two boxlike rooms separated by a narrow hallway, and mostly dark, except for soft, bright beams of light on the art. Several people milled about, gesturing and talking quietly. I glanced around at a few paintings. They looked bizarre—big, swirling patterns of colors and only hints of shapes.

Maribeth greeted us with kisses on both cheeks and bear hugs. I could smell her wildflower smell, and feel her itchy dress through my own sweater; her shaggy collar brushed up against my face. "Ellen, I'm thrilled that you came!" she cried. "You're looking wonderful, honey. The hair is a dream. Well, what do you think? She's Mexican. The artist, I mean."

"I think she's very talented," I said, not at all sure. "I'd like to look around some more."

"Go right ahead. By the way, Sam's stopping by in a few minutes, to bring me some mail I need."

That got me a little nervous. Maribeth was always complaining about her sixteen-year-old son.

I walked slowly through both rooms, liking the darkness,

beginning to like these gorgeous, splashy Mexican colors, and the energy that practically flowed from the canvases. I'd thought I only liked realistic paintings, but it didn't bother me so much, not knowing exactly what these paintings were all about.

A burst of cold air swept through the gallery. It was Sam, letting himself in, holding the door open longer than he needed to.

He looks absolutely ordinary, I thought, as he approached us. A tall, curly-haired kid in a down jacket, plaid shirt, and jeans. But then I noticed puffs of gray hair falling down over his forehead. And he walked awkwardly, leaning too far over to the left. And his left hand was permanently clenched in a curled-up fist. "I couldn't find the envelope," he told Maribeth casually, in a deep, clear voice. Barry would probably never speak so well.

Maribeth's chest expanded, but I could tell she was trying not to get upset. "I told you, on top of the refrigerator—"

"Nope. Never looked there. You never told me."

Loretta rolled her eyes at me. She was saying, This goes on all the time.

"What's happening?" Sam said, looking at Loretta and then over at me. "Are you holding your parents' group here? Those meetings are so stupid! They're only to make you adults feel better!"

He thought I was an adult? He should talk, with all his gray hair!

"Sam," Maribeth said, "I'd like you to meet Ellen, who is Loretta's daughter."

"Oh." Sam looked to the floor. Even in the darkness, a shadow seemed to fall across his face.

"I'm really glad to meet you," I said. Sam grunted. "Are you in high school?"

174

"Of course," Sam told the floor. "What about yourself?"

"Next year." This wasn't so bad. It was still a conversation, even if it was Ellen to Sam to floor. "Are you in a regular school?" I asked.

Sam looked up and glared at me. "Of course I'm in a regular school! What'd you think—I'd be in the circus, with all the other freaks?"

"Oh, God," I said, feeling the blood leave my face. "I'm so sorry." I was as bad as those people in Washington Square Park, as bad as Susie Brockleman—saying the stupid wrong thing at the stupid wrong time.

"Sam is showing you his temper," Maribeth said. "That's enough of a demonstration, Sam. Can we turn it off now?"

Sam plunged the fist of his left hand into the pocket of his jacket and stalked off into the other room.

"I feel like such a dope," I said.

"Don't sweat it, honey," Maribeth said. "Sam's always upset. You just gave him something to pin it on, for the moment."

We all glanced at the other room, still feeling Sam's presence, as if he'd left something of himself in the air.

"Was Sam always this way?" I asked.

"No, honey. Only these last few years. He was the sweetest, most loving child you ever saw."

"You mean, like Barry," I said, and inside I began to crumble.

Loretta put her hand on my arm. "Sam is hardly an exception," she said. "Lots of handicapped adolescents are very unhappy, because they feel so isolated."

I didn't talk for a while, as a thick weight settled in my heart. "It's sad," was all I could think of to say. "I feel like part of me will be sad for the rest of my life."

"Tell me about it!" Maribeth grinned.

175

I looked into her round, dark eyes, and asked, "Doesn't it ever stop feeling sad?"

"Not completely, honey. But you shouldn't try to fight the sadness—it's impossible, it wins every time. And you can't pretend it isn't there, because it is. So you learn to live with it. As if it were a plaid hat. You wear the silly thing."

I walked into the other room, over to Sam. He'd taken off his jacket and had draped it over his fist. "I like that one," I said, pointing to the painting Sam stood in front of. "Do you like it?"

"I don't like any of them." But his tone wasn't as hostile as before.

"Why not?"

"Because they don't mean anything, that's why."

"But they do—they do mean something. They're feelings." I sounded completely confident, and what did I know? Besides, I hadn't even realized this was in my head, before saying it. "The artist wanted to paint her feelings, and this is how they appeared. She probably doesn't understand them completely, either. Sometimes people never understand their feelings."

Sam frowned at the painting, mulling this over. "Show me!" he demanded. "Show me a feeling."

I pointed to a red-black swirl. "There, that's anger."

"And I suppose you think that's jealousy," Sam said, pointing to a muddy, plantlike patch, "and that's pride"— bright gold, almost heart-shaped—"and that's fear"—a swirling white mass pierced by feathery streaks of green. Sam was pointing and pointing and pointing, his face alive with purpose. Now he looked like a son of Maribeth's.

PART FOUR

The Gray Area

12

Robert left home in December . . . and Barry didn't shatter into a million pieces. Maybe because Barry was too busy learning new words: *more, sleepy, Barry, nap, duck, bye-bye, hungry*. Both Claire and Loretta had trouble with Barry's thick nasal sounds. I was always the one who understood them first and had to translate them for everybody else.

My time with Barry kept going by too fast, leaving me way too much time without him. And I wasn't studying as hard as before—it didn't bother me, getting an eighty or even a seventy-five. I started reading a couple of books that I'd skipped when they were assigned in school— *Jane Eyre* and *Wuthering Heights*. These were books that were written because two English girls learned how to write after giving their only brother a box of toy wooden soldiers. I think what happened was that when they played with the soldiers, they got the idea they could play with made-up characters and write a book. It got me thinking, Where were my toy wooden soldiers?

I took a walk one snowy Tuesday afternoon, up

to Shakespeare and Company, a bookstore on Broadway in Greenwich Village. Skimming the shelves, I heard a voice behind me say, "Hi, stranger!"

I spun around. It was Roz Spinak. She still had clear, smooth, glowing skin. Her almond-shaped, light brown eyes were shining. So was her almost-black hair. She was like a Christmas tree, all lit up. "You look terrific," I said.

"Thanks, so do you," she said back, easily. "Late bloomers like us appreciate it more, right? My father always tells me, be glad you weren't born beautiful, be glad you grew into it." She shrugged. "Not that I think I'm beautiful. You know how fathers talk."

No, not really. But I nodded, anyway. Hard to believe this was the same shy, awkward Roz Spinak. "Your father's right," I said. "You are beautiful."

"Stop it!" she said with a laugh. "Listen, come with me to find a book, okay? It's by Roz Chast."

"Who?"

"Ellie, how could you not know who Roz Chast is? She's my idol! She's a wonderful cartoonist. I'm studying to be a cartoonist. That's why I go to Music and Art. Come on, we'll look in Humor."

The High School of Music and Art was a public school, but you had to compete to get in and be really good at something. Roz grabbed the sleeve of my down jacket, and led the way. No one had ever called me "Ellie" before. I liked it.

"Here it is," Roz said. "*Unscientific Americans*. I've got all her other books but not this one. Take a look."

I flipped through the pages and started laughing. There were small, gray, very compressed, and slightly odd drawings of cats in pajamas, Sigmund Freud as a dinosaur, and cartons of milk "turning."

"I love the way she draws," Roz said. "It's almost as if the people know they're getting drawn and aren't sure they like the idea. Even the objects can look self-conscious and uncomfortable."

"I like 'The Humblest Pie of Them All,'" I said. Roz peered over my shoulder at what a deep-dish apple pie was saying: "I'm just a silly old pie! It's not me, it's the ingredients! Shucks, there's *lots* better pies around! Aw, you're embarrassing me!"

"Didn't I tell you?" Roz said. "She's a riot."

"Look at this," I said. There was a drawing on another page of a woman with short, dark, curly hair, and a pinched scowl. The label called her a "non-mobile unit." "It's so weird, she looks just like my Aunt Beryl, but the expression is exactly like my grandmother Anne!"

"I guess they're not two of your favorite relatives," Roz said. "Are they?"

I tried to describe my aunt and my grandmother, but only came up with a few stories about either one—about how Aunt Beryl slept in my bed whenever she visited, and always claimed to be dead, or fractionally dead. That Grandmother Anne gave you back the same gift you'd given her two years before. But I was much more interested in talking to Roz about Roz. "It's strange, isn't it," I said, "you've got the same name as your idol. It's not a common name, either."

"Actually, can you keep a secret?" Roz said, but didn't wait for the answer. "My real name is Rose."

"You're kidding! Rose? But that's pretty."

"I never liked it. I discovered Roz Chast in sixth grade, and changed my name just before junior high."

I admired it—it was kind of a nervy thing to do. "Doesn't your mother mind?" I asked.

181

Roz just blinked at me.

"Oh, I'm sorry, I forgot. Was your mother alive back then?" Why did I have to say the stupid wrong thing twice?

But Roz smiled a half smile. "Actually, she loved the name Roz, and thought it suited me much better than Rose did. She wished she could go back in time and change it, so I could have been Roz all along."

"Well, you're Roz from now on. Infinity only has to extend in one direction." This came out of me before I even understood what it meant.

"Oh, Ellie," Roz said. "I like that! Listen, I've got to go home now, and feed my cat and make dinner for me and my father. Want to come over? We're having spaghetti in garlic, and Häagen-Dazs ice cream."

"Sounds great," I said. But then I remembered that this was Tuesday, one of only two nights all week I could put Barry to bed. If I missed it, there'd only be Thursday night; but when would I accidentally run into Roz again? "I'll have to call my mother," I said, "just to let her know."

Roz paid for the book, and we walked several blocks up Broadway, and several blocks over on Eighth Street, to a gray six-story walk-up apartment building. Roz lived on the second floor. Her apartment was big and sprawling, with high ceilings, framed museum posters on the walls, and oriental rugs. There was a fireplace in the living room, and also a round wooden table, a coffee table piled high with magazines, a TV on an orange crate, a couch, and several big easy chairs with threads dangling. "My cat, Smoky, has ruined every chair in the place," Roz said, throwing our jackets over the TV. "She doesn't just scratch them, either. She slices holes in the fabric on the bottom so she can crawl inside and curl up in the springs. She crawls inside the springs in my bed too and shakes it in the middle of the night. But she sits in my lap when I draw, and she's a real beauty. You might not get to see her. She gets all sulky around strangers. Go ahead, call your mother, I'll give Smoky her dry food."

I dialed Loretta's number at the library. When I told her I wasn't coming home for dinner, she sounded almost thrilled. "Will you kiss Barry good night for me?" I asked, and Loretta said she would.

Roz and I went through a winding hall to her room in the back. It was a mess, with clothes and books scattered all over, and art posters covering her walls like wallpaper, and a couple of flannel shirts hanging over her mirror. But her art desk—a slanted white board with pens stacked neatly at the top—was all clean and clear and waiting for her.

She dumped a load of stuff off her bed, and showed me a patchwork quilt underneath. It had windmills, and roses with big thorns, and glittering stars like diamonds in a black sky. "My grandmother made this," Roz said. "She died when I was three. See the thorns? My father said she was a big believer in thorns. Not that you should go sticking your fingers on them. Just that you shouldn't ever forget they exist."

I ran my hands over the quilt. These thorns were soft. "It's beautiful," I said. "My grandmother never made anything for anybody." What was it about Roz, I wondered, that made me want to tell her things?

Roz gave me another half smile. Then she said, "Oh, hear the growl? Smoky's inside the bed, growling at you."

So I leaned under the bed and growled right back at the noise.

"Well, that surprised her! She just stopped!" Roz said. "Look, I want to show you some of my work, but only if you'll give me your honest opinion."

I sat on the bed, and Roz handed me two cartoons. Right away I could see that Roz Spinak was very talented, even if she was imitating Roz Chast a little bit. Beneath a drawing of a skinny, towering girl with a powerfully defiant look in her eyes, and wearing a polka-dot dress, Roz wrote: "Never mind the fashion, Arlene had to wear polka dots, and she did." The other cartoon portrayed two identical men with broad, stooped shoulders and porcupine-stiff hair, with the caption, "Twins, not separated at birth."

"My honest opinion is, your stuff is terrific," I said. Roz nodded, seeing I meant it. "The stoop of the shoulders on the twins is very good. It makes them look all paranoid and defensive. And I like the look in Arlene's eyes. My mother had that same look, about a year and a half ago."

"Thanks, Ellie," Roz said. "Why did your mother have that look in her eyes?"

I stared up at one of Roz's posters: a blossoming almond branch, by van Gogh. Delicate pink-white flowers on dark, gnarled, twisty branches, against a brilliant blue sky. I wanted to tell Roz things, but sometimes I couldn't actually do it. "I don't remember," I said.

Roz looked at me a moment, and this time gave me a big smile. "Come on," she said. "Let's make dinner. I hope you like lots of garlic."

Roz's father came home just before seven o'clock, as he did every night, according to Roz. He was adorable—short and cuddly-looking, with a fuzzy brown beard, fuzzy eyebrows, lots of fuzzy brown hair, and eyes that were small and round and widely set apart, like a koala bear's. He shook my hand inside both of his. They were so warm, his hands. "I'm Walter Spinak," he said, his eyes crinkling up.

We all sat at the round wooden table in the living room, eating steamy and very garlicky spaghetti. Eighth Street was noisy, even with the windows closed, I heard buses wheezing, police sirens whooping, ambulances wailing, car alarms screaming, car radios blasting music, and kids shouting and laughing.

"The only quiet time is Sunday morning," Walter Spinak said. "And even then the car alarms go off."

But I liked it here, crazy noise and all.

"What year of school are you in?" Walter Spinak asked me.

"Ninth grade," I answered. "I'll be graduating this year, sir."

"Please don't call me that! Plain old Walt will do."

I tried to picture Robert saying, Just call me plain old Bob. Not in a million years!

"So," Walt said, "do you live nearby? Do you have any brothers or sisters?"

"I live in Soho," I answered. "I have a brother. He's . . . very young. He'll be two in February."

"The terrible twos," Walt said. "They're hell at that age. Running all over the place. Demanding that things be done exactly their way."

"Yes," I said. I'm sorry, I was telling Barry in my head, but I can't talk about you yet. Please don't ask why. "My mother's a librarian, over on Sixth Avenue. My father's . . . in Connecticut."

Walt's fuzzy eyebrows rose up. "Do you get to see him at all?"

"Oh," I said, realizing what I'd made it sound like. "My parents aren't divorced or anything. He comes home a few times a year. He just works up there, in Connecticut."

"But why does he work there?" Walt said.

I twirled around some spaghetti. "Business," I said. "I don't really understand it."

"Why don't you leave Ellie alone?" Roz broke in. "Her food's getting cold."

"I don't mind," I said. "Look, I'm almost finished, anyway." I liked having Walter Spinak ask me questions, even when I wasn't able to answer them.

"So, what are you interested in, Ellen?" he asked me next. "Any particular careers in mind?"

"Not really," I said. "I guess the answer is no, sir—I mean, no, Walt."

"Surely you're interested in something," he said. "What are your choices?"

"Choices," I said, as if I'd never heard the word. "It's hard to explain. I don't have any choices. I mean, my future doesn't feel . . . real. It doesn't feel like anything." I didn't know how strange this would sound, until I'd heard it said out loud. A blush began to creep up my neck.

"Don't you worry, Ellie," Roz said. "We'll get you a future. We'll figure something out for you—something worthy of your talent."

I felt I had just been given a pre-Christmas present, and it was wonderful. But could I open it now? I wondered. Yes, a voice inside me said, but don't go ripping into the paper. Open it slowly, carefully.

"Time for dessert," Roz announced. I helped her pick up plates, and followed her into the kitchen. She took a pint of chocolate chocolate-chip ice cream out of the freezer, and dug a big spoon into it. "This stuff has about a million

186

calories," she said. "And it's so expensive! Guess how much it cost."

A little car alarm went off in my head. Was Roz hinting, the way Mrs. Needleman had hinted at me a long time ago?

"Roz," I said. "I'll be happy to . . . put in something. I've got some with me, in my jacket. Do you have any particular place for it?"

"Ellie, what are you talking about?"

Mist swirled over the ice cream. "I thought maybe you wanted me to help out, and share the expense—"

"You thought I wanted your money?" Roz put a hand to her mouth.

"Well, I used to be friends with this girl named Faye Needleman. I ate dinner over there a lot, and her mother complained that fried chicken TV dinners cost so much, and they both thought I should put money in their cookie jar. So I did."

Roz started to laugh. "Oh, Ellie," she said. "That's so sad it's funny."

I started laughing too. Because it was so sad.

The three of us ate ice cream, and played a couple of games of Scrabble where nobody kept score. Afterward, Walt went off to do some reading, and Roz and I did the dishes—she washed, I dried.

"Your father's so nice," I said. Not that I ever brought friends home, but I knew Robert would never sit around and play games with them.

"Don't let my father fool you," Roz said. "He can be such a pain. For instance, he writes me letters. Here we are, living under the same roof, and he mails me these long, chatty letters. And expects me to write him back!"

That didn't sound so bad. Actually it sounded friendly. "What kind of work does he do?"

"He's a doctor."

I liked that too. He didn't go around bragging, "I'm a doctor, you see." No, he was just plain old Walt.

Soon it was time to go. I stood at Roz's front door, not sure how to tell her how much fun I'd had. The feeble way it came out was, "Thanks, Roz."

"You're welcome. Listen, let's get together over the weekend, okay? Go to a movie or something."

"Yes, definitely," I said. Roz didn't say which day she had in mind, and I thought, Who will I be giving up this weekend—Loretta or Barry?

As Roz and I exchanged phone numbers on little slips of paper, a sleek gray cat with radiant green eyes appeared at my feet, and rubbed up against me.

"She likes you!" Roz cried. "I'm amazed."

"Because I growled at her," I said.

"But I like you, and you didn't growl at me," Roz said mildly. "Not recently, anyway. Not that I ever really held it against you." And with that, Roz put what had happened two years ago behind us. "I'll go get my father. He'll never let you walk home alone."

On the way back to Soho, light snow fell, slow and dreamy, and gave the streets a powdered-sugar look.

"That boarded-up Burger King on your left used to be a great bookstore, three floors of books," Walt told me. "The triplex we just passed, with the three terrible movies? Used to be a big-screen theater that showed only art films. Once upon a time, this was a supermarket. Now it's a bunch of shoe stores. If there's one thing Eighth Street doesn't need, it's more shoe stores."

I loved hearing Walt ramble on about the changes in his neighborhood. A car swerved around a corner really fast, and Walt threw his arm around me, pulling me back from the curb. Why don't you adopt me? I was thinking. I could move in tomorrow.

When I got home, I thought maybe Loretta had forgotten to do it for me, so I kissed Barry good night as he slept.

Robert and Loretta were talking about me at dinner, with me sitting right there, feeding Barry. It was around Christmas, and Robert had come home for a few days.

"Ellen looks happier," Robert said.

"Ellen's got a new friend," Loretta told him. "Ellen's spent the last two weeks with her, including Sundays. I'm thinking of changing Sunday on the calendar to 'Ellen and Roz's Day!' " But Loretta was smiling.

"Her name is Roz?" Robert asked.

"Roz Spinak," Loretta said. "She goes to the High School of Music and Art, and she wants to be a cartoonist. This is what Ellen's told me—I haven't met her yet."

"I'd very much like to meet her," Robert said.

"Swallow," I told Barry. I could never explain it to them, how Roz Spinak was an entirely separate part of my life, and how I wanted to keep it that way for as long as I could. "Roz is very busy right now," I said. "She'd like to come over. She's said so lots of times. But I can't do it yet—I mean, she can't do it yet, for at least a month."

"When I'll be away," Robert said—a little sadly, I thought.

The phone rang way too early on a Saturday morning. It was the first weekend of the new year. "Hello," I said groggily, and heard Aunt Beryl tell me, "You weren't sleeping."

189

I guess this was her way of asking if I'd been asleep. "It's all right," I said. "I would've gotten up in three hours, anyway."

"Oh, Ellen, stop joking," Aunt Beryl said. "Please tell your mother I'll be spending the night there tonight." Click.

What a way to wake up.

"I'm more than dead—I'm buried," Aunt Beryl said when she arrived that night, dropping her gray overnight bag on the floor with a thud. She wore her long dark-plum down coat zipped up from her ankles to her throat. "The *traffic*. You'd think the whole world had to drive into New York City tonight."

I picked up Aunt Beryl's bag—it felt so heavy—and brought it to my room. When I got back, Aunt Beryl had sunk into an easy chair, and Loretta was saying, "I've completely forgotten about something very important. Ellen and I have to go out tonight."

"What?" Aunt Beryl said.

"What?" I said.

Barry sat on the floor with a puzzle. He looked up, mildly interested.

"A long time ago," Loretta said, "I promised my friend Maribeth that I'd bring Ellen to a special meeting for the siblings of handicapped children. It slipped my mind. It's tonight."

Loretta had never mentioned this to me. "We don't have to go," I said.

"But we do," Loretta insisted. I noticed she was blushing a little.

"I don't think I can watch Barry," Aunt Beryl said. "I'm simply not up to it. Some other night, perhaps, but not tonight."

Loretta was already handing me my jacket. "It has to be tonight," she told Aunt Beryl. "Besides, Barry's nearly asleep. I've already fed him. He'll be no trouble at all. Help yourself to some chicken in the refrigerator."

"But I was hoping we could all stay together," Aunt Beryl said, her lower lip protruding. She looked like a child who'd been spanked.

Once outside in the snappy nighttime air, Loretta hooked her arm through mine, and said, "We're really going to the movies, and then out for hot chocolate."

"What!" I was multiply shocked. "Mom, you just lied to Aunt Beryl!"

She squeezed my arm. "Didn't think I had it in me, did you?"

"Actually, no." I watched her cloudy breath swirl around and disappear. It was only later I remembered she'd once told me that she never lied. I asked her, "Why'd you do it?"

"Because I simply wasn't in an Aunt Beryl mood tonight," she replied. "Because I missed you. You're always going off with your friend Roz, and I wanted to spend an evening with you. Are you hungry? We can stop for a bite on the way."

"Mom, I have a bad feeling about it, leaving Aunt Beryl alone with Barry."

"El, he's probably asleep by now. Besides, he's a tough little kid. Aunt Beryl can't do anything to him."

We went to a revival house on First Avenue, to see an old black-and-white comedy. There was a girl named Ellie in it, and she was running away, and she looked so sad sometimes, listening to train whistles in the dark. And I couldn't stop thinking about Barry.

"Did you like it?" Loretta asked, as we left the theater. "Hey, slow down!"

I was practically running. "It was great. That was a great idea, Mom, going to the movies."

"Yes, I could see how much you enjoyed yourself," Loretta said, rolling her eyes. "*It Happened One Night*, one of the funniest movies ever, and you barely crack a smile. Let's stop for hot chocolate."

"No! I mean, I don't feel like it. I'll make some at home."

"Stop worrying, El. Barry is fine."

But when we got home, Aunt Beryl sat crumpled up on the couch, crying. My throat closed in on itself. "What happened?" I managed to say. Aunt Beryl kept on crying.

Loretta rushed into her room to look at Barry, and came back a moment later, confused. "He's asleep," she said to me. "He's perfectly fine." Then she turned to Aunt Beryl. "What's the matter with you?"

Aunt Beryl's nose was red and her eyes were swollen. "He spoke to me," she said. "I was sitting right here and watching television—a news show." I knew she adored nighttime soaps, but never mind. "I yawned, and Barry said to me, 'Sleepy? Go nap.'"

"That's terrific!" I said, almost busting with pride. "Barry's first sentence. I'm so impressed."

"You don't understand," Aunt Beryl said, with a fresh wave of tears. "I thought Loretta was making it up, when she said Barry could say words. To me it always sounded like so much garbled nonsense. But tonight he spoke to me. He . . . was concerned, because I was tired. For the first time I saw the sweet child inside that body."

So, Aunt Beryl and I shared a talent. We were the ones who could understand Barry's words on the first try. Loretta and I made Aunt Beryl some hot chocolate, and sat with her as she took long sips and cried it out. By the time Aunt Beryl curled up in my bed, she was close to smiling. Poor

Aunt Beryl, I thought. She'd had a bad shock—as bad as if the toaster had started tap dancing.

The next morning, I saw Aunt Beryl fresh from the shower, wrapped in Loretta's white terry-cloth bathrobe. I noticed a thin red line on her forehead, from a too-small shower cap. "Ellen, I don't know how you sleep at night, she said. "That snoring! From such a tiny child. It's no wonder my eyes are so puffy, I couldn't sleep a wink. And then earlier this morning, just when I was drifting off, he crawled into my room and started babbling away at me. Lord only knows what he thought he was saying—I couldn't decipher a syllable. By the way, I might have used the last of the hot water. When I finished my shower, it felt icy cold."

Why did I feel disappointed? Had I really expected a nonmobile unit like Aunt Beryl to change?

After omelets, which Aunt Beryl had called "perfect, if a little dry," Aunt Beryl cornered me as I washed the breakfast dishes in lukewarm water.

"Your father will be home in March, if I'm not mistaken?" Her voice held a hint of something else, the way an autumn breeze suddenly feels like winter. "It's so wonderful that he and Loretta have stayed married all this time. So many couples come to grief because the husband is in the military. And so many marriages fall apart over the stress of raising a handicapped child. And so many marriages simply peter out after about fifteen years. Imagine—Robert and Loretta have been together for sixteen years."

I stood at the sink, rinsing off soapy plates, and waited for Aunt Beryl's words to twist up my insides. But nothing happened. "They'll never get divorced, Aunt Beryl," I said.

Aunt Beryl pulled the sash of Loretta's bathrobe, tying it tightly around herself. "I couldn't agree more," she said.

193

"They won't be like those couples who seem so perfect for each other, right up to the day they separate, shocking everybody—"

"They love each other too much," I cut her off.

Aunt Beryl touched the red line on her forehead, and said, "I'm sure you're right. Of course, who's to say what love is, exactly?"

Poor Aunt Beryl. She had lost her power over me, and we both knew it.

13

Roz and I sat in a booth, sipping Cokes and sharing french fries smothered in ketchup. We were in a coffee shop in Greenwich Village, one of those places you can find in New York that looks absolutely ordinary, with tall padded stools, a long L-shaped Formica-top counter facing a row of griddles, red plastic-covered booths down the walls, and wax flowers in the window—but where the food is fantastic. "Roz, I'd like to invite you over next Sunday," I said. "For a birthday party. *My* birthday party. I'll be fourteen."

"Name the time and I'll be there," Roz said, waving and nodding to our waiter. "I've just asked for another order. I'm starving. Is it dress up?"

"No, it's only me, you, my mother, my mother's friend—her son won't come—and my brother." I knew I couldn't hide my life forever. I knew I had to come out with it, about Barry. And maybe even about Robert too. Several deep breaths didn't help. My nerves were jumping all around. "Roz, my little brother . . . Barry?

There's something about him you should know. He's got cerebral palsy."

"Oh, yeah?" Roz said, not missing a beat. "Okay."

I thought maybe she hadn't heard me right. "He has to walk with a walker," I said, "and even so, he falls down a lot. He can say a whole bunch of words, only it's hard to make them out. But don't worry, I understand him really well."

"I'm not worried, Ellie."

"He might have mental retardation," I went on. "It's hard to tell when a child is this young. Do you know any kids with CP? CP—that's short for cerebral palsy."

"Thanks for telling me, I'd never have figured it out," Roz said, smiling. "No, I don't know any kids with CP. Your brother will be my first. Oh, here they are. I love it when they're so brown on the outside."

"Roz, don't you have any kind of reaction at all?"

"Well . . . I'm looking forward to meeting your little brother. Why, what kind of reaction were you expecting?"

So I told Roz about Faye Needleman, who found out about Barry and then stopped coming over. About Grandmother Anne, who insisted that Barry's handicap remain a secret from my grandfather, because it would kill him to find out. About Aunt Beryl, who still saw Barry as a case of cerebral palsy, even though she'd seen for herself that he was a real little boy.

"Oh, Ellie," Roz said. "You've been through it, haven't you?"

"I invited Aunt Beryl to the party," I said. "But she told me she shouldn't be driving into the city anymore, now that the traffic was so bad."

Roz nodded at me. There was a look in her eyes, as if

she finally understood a few things she'd been confused about.

I nodded back. Two years before, Aunt Beryl had scared me badly, telling me, "Things happen, people disappear." But now she had made herself disappear.

Walking Roz home on Sixth Avenue, I took some more deep breaths. "I guess I should tell you about my father," I said. "It's true that he works in Connecticut. But six months out of the year, he's somewhere out in the ocean, because he's an officer aboard a nuclear submarine."

This time Roz missed a beat. She grabbed the sleeve of my jacket, and her eyes got very wide.

I felt a sudden dull ache in my chest. A handicapped brother—that could touch your heart. But a father who kept sixteen nuclear warheads pointing at the planet?

"I had no idea," Roz breathed out.

"Well, now you have the idea," I said.

"But Ellie, it's fascinating! Tell me all about it. What's it like to be on a submarine? What does he eat? Where does he sleep?"

"Wait a minute," I said. "Doesn't it bother you at all that in about the time it takes me to walk you home my father could destroy half the world?"

"You mean, all by himself?" Roz asked.

"Actually, no," I said. "He has to get orders from the president first, and then four men have to turn four keys simultaneously to launch the missiles." I frowned. "Still, don't you find the whole idea . . . a little monstrous?" Especially when Dr. Walter Spinak goes around saving lives, I was thinking.

"I'm definitely against nuclear weapons, if that's what

you're asking. I think they should all be dismantled and sold for scrap. But your father didn't invent the system, and besides, he probably thinks he's preventing nuclear war. He's not trigger-happy, is he?"

I shook my head. "He doesn't ever want to fire the missiles. He says the whole point is to keep us at peace."

"Ellie, he's not monstrous just because the world is that way. Now tell me all about the submarine. Have you ever been on board?"

She reminded me of myself, when I was little, asking my father millions of questions. "No, his submarine docks in Scotland," I said. "But I know all about it, anyway." As we walked on, I told Roz that the officers and crew eat very well, because the food is prepared by French-trained gourmet chefs; that my father shares a tiny cabin with one other officer; that he's got access to an exercise room, with treadmills and Nautilus machines, and a recreation room with VCRs and loads of movies, and an ice-cream machine that's on twenty-four hours a day.

"I can't believe you never told me this before," Roz said. "You might be the only girl in New York City who can say her father works on a nuclear submarine."

"That's probably true. Most of the submarine crews live in Connecticut. We only moved to New York because of my grandparents."

"You amaze me," Roz said. "You're unique, but you're trying to seem ordinary."

I opened my mouth, but no words came out.

"I'd love to meet your father," Roz said.

No, you wouldn't, I thought. He's not like Walt. "That'll be great," I said. "Of course, he's not home all that often."

"I know," Roz said, tossing her head back and giving me

a sideways smile. "You already told me. Come on up and say hello to Smoky. Last time you left, she howled by the front door."

New people can be very scary," Roz said to Barry when she met him. But is it okay if I sit next to you?" Barry, who was sitting on the carpet, looking adorable in a blue polo shirt and blue stretch pants, nodded that it was okay.

Loretta, who had put on an emerald green sweatshirt and black jeans, brought in a chocolate cake with fourteen flickering candles. Then Roz picked up Barry and held him in her lap while everybody sang "Happy Birthday." I blew out the candles and had real trouble making a wish, because for the moment everything I liked was right there in the room.

Maribeth gave me some wildflower perfume. "Only a few drops, and you can feel out in the country, even when stuck on the subway," she said. Loretta handed me a fifty-dollar gift certificate from Lord & Taylor, with a card from Robert that said, "All my love, always." I wondered what brought that on. Usually he just signed it, "Love." Barry said, "Barry loves Nellie"—or close enough. "We've been working on this at UCP," Loretta said, laughing. "Vs are so tough for Barry. At one point all the kids in his class were saying 'Barry loves Nellie!' " Roz told me she would give me my gift in private.

We sat around talking and eating lasagna and salad, cake and ice cream and drinking lemonade and hot chocolate. Roz put a bib on Barry and fed him some ice cream, and barely flinched when most of it came right back out again. On our trips to the kitchen, Loretta and Maribeth each separately pulled me aside to say how much they liked Roz, and Roz pulled me aside to say how much she liked everybody else, especially Loretta. "She's so pretty," Roz said. "She's got a real spark in her."

"Oh, yeah?" I said. "I always thought that about Maribeth."

"Oh, Maribeth is terrific," Roz said. "But your mother's got such strength, and she loves you so much."

I wasn't used to occasions that were fun all the way through with no bumpy spots.

When it was time for Barry's nap, Loretta and Maribeth took care of the cleanup, and Roz and I went into my room.

Roz pulled something out of a shopping bag and handed it to me. It was a piece of white cardboard, about the size of an album cover, with a big brightly colored pie graph in the middle, divided into about fifty slices, each labeled with a profession. I could see Teacher, Lawyer, Art Critic, Psychiatrist—but there were far too many to take in all at once. There was a spinner glued to the center, with a tiny arrow at its tip. All around the graph, there were drawings of me, looking thoughtful—pretty flattering portraits, actually—with puffy, dreamy question marks floating nearby. It must have taken her two days to make this.

"It's just . . . amazingly amazing," I said.

"It's a start, anyway," Roz said. "Go on, give it a spin."

I came up with Dog Groomer, and then Brain Surgeon, and, after that, Astronaut.

"I left a couple of spaces blank so you can fill in whatever you want. Happy birthday, Ellie."

I gave her a hug. What else was there to say?

Roz settled into my rocking chair, sitting Indian-style, as I stretched out on the bed. It was almost dusk. Rumbly snoring could be heard from the next room. "Is that Barry?"

Roz said, and I nodded. "Ellie, where does Barry go to school?"

"Right now he's in the Infant Stimulation Program at United Cerebral Palsy," I said. "In a few weeks, when he's two years old he'll go into their preschool program. When he turns six, he can be mainstreamed—meaning, he ll go into a regular elementary school and take special-education classes."

"That'll be hard on him, won't it? To be around all the other kids, and know that he's different."

"Yes," I said.

"I know what that's like," Roz said. "Feeling different, every instant of every day."

The turtle started splashing around in his tank. He got superactive sometimes. "You mean, because of your mother?"

"Because my mother had cancer," she said. "Because she was sick for only five months, but it felt like five years. Because every day in school, I got worried that I'd go home to find her sicker. And every night, I'd be scared to go to sleep, afraid to find her sicker again when I woke up. Because after she died, when Ms. Stapler stood up in front of the class and announced it, some kids snickered at me. Some called me an orphan, though technically I was only half an orphan." She smiled at that, but I could tell she might start to cry. "It was such a relief, going to Music and Art, where I was a stranger to everybody." I leaned over to the rocking chair, and held her hand—it felt dry and warm. "For so long, I hated her, Ellie," Roz said softly. "I hated her for getting sick and dying on me."

"Mmm," I said.

Couldn't I do any better than that? Why wasn't it taught in school—how to be a friend? But then I realized I could do better. "You didn't really hate her, Roz," I said. "You only hated her sickness, and the way it was making you feel."

Roz looked at me steadily. "Maybe," she said. "Because I don't hate her so much anymore, and she's still dead— wow, that sounds strange."

"Not to me," I said. "I mean, I know what it's like to hate somebody for something that isn't their fault. I had to hate Barry before I could let myself love him."

And Roz said, "Sometimes I think I have to learn how to love my mother all over again."

I turned that over in my head. I'd always thought you knew how to love the way you knew how to blink—automatically. But maybe getting it right was something you had to learn.

"Tell me about your mother," I said, "before she got sick."

Roz's light brown eyes glistened, but she wasn't crying. "Well, she had red hair," she said. "Not as dark as Maribeth's—more like the orange-red you see in campfires." Roz told me that her mother had very pale skin and a long, pretty neck, and she sang a lot, really badly. She loved mysteries—she could read three a day—and she always forgot the punch lines to jokes, which always made them even funnier. "She had one really beautiful dress, made of green chiffon," Roz said. "When you hugged her in this dress, it made a sound, like crunchy leaves."

Barry in preschool meant that Barry was now in a classroom with a bunch of new classmates and a bunch of new teachers, and no Loretta. So Loretta went back to working at the library full-time. Claire picked Barry up in the afternoons, and came home with him on the UCP bus.

A couple of Saturdays, Roz wheeled Barry around in his stroller, and helped him use his walker. Whenever people stared at Barry, Roz was horrified. "I don't know how you stand it, Ellie," she said. But she got used to it faster than I did, and by the end of the second Saturday she was staring back at the starers.

A couple of Sundays, Roz joined me and Loretta on our outings. Once we went to the conservatory in the Bronx Botanical Gardens—a huge, domed, glass greenhouse built at the turn of the century. In a room filled entirely with ferns, Loretta and Roz started telling each other some of the dumbest jokes I'd ever heard. I felt completely happy, listening to them laugh, surrounded by the smell of damp earth, and gigantic green, glossy ferns.

In the middle of March, Robert, who was home for the month, put up Sheetrock walls in the living room and created an entirely new room, for Barry. Now the living room had a big square cut into it, but this didn't ruin the feeling of the loft—the living room had looked way too big, anyway. When Robert asked Barry what color he wanted for his walls, Barry pointed to my room and told him, "Nelliebuhll," (which I knew meant "blue walls, just like Nellie's"). Loretta put Barry's first real bed, with a rail along one side, in one corner of his new room. Robert constructed a shelf for the turtle, and I gave Barry my duck lamp, which got put on top of a bureau covered entirely with silky quilted fabric.

With all this work in the loft, I didn't see much of Roz that month, and besides, she was taking her midterms. Several times Robert asked me when he could finally meet Roz. I kept telling him, "We'll find a good time"—and then changed the subject. Every time I did see Roz, I sort of forgot to tell her that Robert was around.

I tried out for softball in April.

"Look who's here!" Ms. Moore greeted me. "So, Missy Ellen Gray thinks she can just show up and all is forgiven!"

I hadn't thought she'd be so mad at me, for not even trying out last season. "I want to play third base," I said.

"Listen to her! That's strike one, Ellen," she said, smirking at me. She put me up against all her best batters, and I was a little rusty, but even when fumbling I managed to get hold of the ball and throw it all the way to first. When the positions were posted three days later, Susie Brockleman was placed way out in center field—and I got third base. I knew Ms. Moore would be extra tough on me all season, but I hardly cared. Third base. It felt like returning home.

Roz came to watch a game one afternoon in Central Park. It was late May, a typical New York "almost summer" day— hot in the sunshine, chilly in the shadows of trees.

We lost, 6–4.

Somehow Ms. Moore made each girl feel it was solely her own fault. This was Ms. Moore's talent. Everybody looked gloomy, except for Susie Brockleman. A losing game never affected her, even though in this case the loss was mostly because of her.

As Roz and I walked off the field, I noticed Ray Frost heading straight for us. He can't have come all this way just to talk to me, I thought, getting completely excited anyway. But if he did, I'll be so friendly he won't know what hit him.

But he veered off and walked by, without even glancing at me. I turned around to see Susie Brockleman, her curly hair lustrous in the sunlight, place her hands behind Ray Frost's neck and reach up to kiss him.

"I don't believe it," I said to Roz. "First Susie Brockleman throws the ball to second and hits the runner. Then she swings at pitches that look more like gutter balls in bowling and strikes out. And now she's seeing a guy I like!"

"That blond guy? Ellie, you never told me."

"I don't think I knew it, until now. He was so nice to me one day, months ago, but I really blew it."

We curved around a dirt path lined with tall, lush trees that smelled minty sweet. "Well, you never know," Roz said.

I tried picturing Ray Frost dialing my number and asking me out, but the image wouldn't take shape. "I'm not holding my breath," I said.

"Look, Susie Brockleman played third base last year, and you got that back, didn't you? Wonderful things do happen."

But the bad mood I was in wasn't getting any better. "Some things aren't wonderful at all," I said, "and they stay not-wonderful forever. Look at Barry, for instance. Look at Barry and what he has to live with for the whole rest of his life."

"That's true," Roz said. "Barry's opened your eyes. He's spared you the illusion that life is just a bowl of blueberries."

"Cherries," I corrected her.

"But Barry's also a good kid," Roz went on, "even inside his not-so-wonderful situation. And anyway all the bad stuff put together can't stop wonderful things from happening."

Maybe it was my mood, but I couldn't help thinking, They just can't last, those wonderful things Roz believes in so strongly.

We came out of the park and crossed Central Park West, on our way to the subway. Roz said, "Listen, I have news.

205

I've been accepted at a really good art camp in Maine, and I'll be going away for the whole summer."

I stood statue-still. So, congratulate her, I told myself. Give her a big hug. Tell her you're so happy for her.

Instead I busted out crying.

"What is it, what's wrong?" Roz said, wrapping her arm around me.

I kept on crying, across the street from the Museum of Natural History. Several people glanced at me and quickly looked the other way. It sort of fascinated me that there were people who could stare endlessly at a child with a walker, while others politely turn away when a fourteen-year-old girl sobs in the street. "I'll miss you," I said.

"But I'll miss you too. Tell me another reason."

"That's the only reason! You're going away."

"Well, Ellie, I think it goes deeper than that," Roz said. "All I can tell you is that we'll still be best friends when I get back."

I cried some more, thinking, Maybe some wonderful things can last.

Loretta sat with all the other parents in the center of the auditorium, and watched me graduate from junior high school.

There wasn't much to see. All the ninth-graders piled into the side seats. Nobody wore caps and gowns—some kids even wore jeans. I had on a skirt and blouse. Basically, some eighth-graders played some brass instruments, and your name was called and you marched up onstage for your diploma. It was just a sheet of paper, not rolled up in a red ribbon or anything.

Afterward, everybody went to the gym to hug everybody

else. I did a lot more watching than hugging, since I really hadn't gotten too friendly with anybody except Roz.

"You miss Roz, don't you?" Loretta asked me.

"And how," I answered. She'd left for camp several days before.

"She called last week, when you weren't home," Loretta said. "We had a wonderful talk. Did she mention it to you?" I shook my head. "I even miss her a little myself," she added.

All around me, I heard kids tell each other, "Don't ever change." What a strange thing to say to anybody just out of ninth grade.

I managed to get a few hugs, before the day ended. I'll never know why, but when Susie Brockleman cried into my shoulder, I found myself crying too. And I was still crying when Ms. Stapler put her arms around me, with Loretta standing nearby. I thought Ms. Stapler might be nearly in tears herself, but she said, "It's my contacts. They seem to bother me every graduation day." Ms. Stapler was starting to grow on me.

When it was almost time to go home, I noticed Muriel Nash standing by herself under a basketball hoop. Her hair was long again, and hung limply around her neck. She wore a shiny, too-tight, green silk dress—I could see the bumps of her bra straps and the elastic on her panty hose. "Mom, I'll be right back," I said, and walked over to Muriel.

"Well, hi," I said to her. "How've you been?"

Muriel shrugged. "I'm so-so," she said, still spitting a little on the *s*'s. "But you probably want to hear about Faye, am I right?"

I looked around. "She's here somewhere, isn't she?"

"How could she be? She dropped out of school."

"What! That's impossible. Don't you have to be sixteen?"

Muriel shrugged again. "Faye's fourteen, same as you and me. A few months ago, she moved out to her sister's place in California. She smudged up a Xerox of her birth certificate, and went to high school for a while. She even did all right, but then she dropped out. Her sister backed her up. Sylvie went to the school authorities and said Faye was needed at home."

"I'm really sorry to hear it," I said.

"Don't be," Muriel said. "She's happy. She's a waitress at Denny's and she meets cute guys at every meal. Feel sorry for me, if you want to feel sorry for somebody. I'm all alone now."

I'd been dealing with a little aloneness too. "You want to get together sometime?" I asked Muriel.

"I don't think so." Muriel flattened her hair over her right eye. "We're still mad at you. You dropped us like we were nothing."

"That was a long time ago," I said. "Things are different now." We're different now, I wanted to say.

But Muriel was holding on to Faye, even though Faye was three thousand miles away. Muriel turned her back on me. "We have nothing to say to you," she said, over her shoulder. Her legs made a swishing sound as she walked away.

14

"Grandmother Anne called. She needs a favor."
I was drifting in and out of sleep when I heard
Loretta's voice.

"You've got to pick up a prescription for her,
El. I'm so sorry about this. I'd go myself if I didn't
have to work."

I sat up. Washed by morning sunlight, Loretta
stood leaning against my doorway, in an about-
to-go-to-work blouse and skirt. This person is my
mother, I thought dreamily, happily. Of all the
millions of possibilities.

But then what she was saying hit me. "You
mean I'm supposed to go all the way up to Washington Heights for a prescription? Isn't there a
drugstore right near the home?"

"Yes, several," Loretta said, rolling her eyes.
"Anne won't go out at all nowadays—the neighborhood frightens her. And I'll make it worse for
you. Some teenage boys from a local high school
do volunteer work for the home. All Anne has to
do is call the office and ask that one of the boys
run the errand for her."

"Then why doesn't she?"

"She doesn't want the boys knowing her business."

"As if they would care!" I was fully awake now, filled with the outrageousness of the situation. "What's the prescription for, anyway?"

"Anne wouldn't say. Sleeping pills, probably. Maybe tranquilizers."

And Grandmother Anne had criticized my mother for taking drugs. "Okay, I'll do it this once," I grumbled. "But never again."

"You'll probably never have to. Beryl usually does it, Anne explained to me, but Beryl is ill."

"What's wrong with Aunt Beryl?"

Loretta said, "Flu."

I heard it as "flew."

It was July first, a steamy and drippingly hot Monday. I wore as little as possible—shorts and a halter—and, carrying a loaf of fresh rye bread that Loretta had bought at the bakery, made my way uptown on an air-conditioned subway car. Once I was back out into the heat, I picked up Grandmother Anne's prescription in a stapled-shut white bag.

When I knocked on their door, Grandfather Mitchell answered. "Anne is lying down," he whispered. "Come in, I've got the air on." He meant the air conditioner.

"Here's some rye bread," I said, straining to speak loud enough for him to hear me, but soft enough not to wake up Grandmother Anne.

"Mmm, it smells delicious. Sit, dear, you must be tired after your long ride. What'll it be—iced tea or lemonade?"

"Iced tea."

I tried settling into one of their stiff plastic chairs, but it wasn't easy—the plastic kept sticking to my legs and back.

The room was dim; maroon curtains covered the windows. Grandfather Mitchell handed me a tall glass of iced tea with a single, cloudy ice cube in it (they only had a tiny refrigerator, with a miniature freezer that didn't work too well). He sat down across from me, wearing a short-sleeved, clingy white polo shirt and brown slacks.

"How is Barry?" he asked.

Don't tell! Don't tell! I could hear Grandmother Anne's voice in my head. Or was it Aunt Beryl's? "Barry is absolutely fine," I said.

"That is, for a child with cerebral palsy," Grandfather Mitchell said calmly, gazing at me with friendly brown eyes.

I sipped some iced tea. It tasted powdery. Of course he knew. He'd known from the beginning, the same way Loretta had. Then why was I so surprised? Why did my voice break a little when I said, "So I guess you know"?

"I suspected it at first. Barry was so limp and quiet. The fact that it was cerebral palsy I couldn't help overhearing. Anne and Beryl speak on the phone quite often. Long conversations."

I nodded. That part didn't surprise me at all. "Barry uses a walker at home," I said. "He works with a therapist every day—she's wonderful with him." Grandfather Mitchell smiled fondly. He'd heard me just fine. So how many times had he heard himself described as "deaf as a post"? "Grandpa, why does Grandma hide information from you, information that doesn't hurt you at all?"

He shrugged. "It's just her way," he said.

Way of what? I wanted to say. "I don't think it's right," I told him.

"Don't judge Anne too harshly, dear. She's had a tough life. She was the only daughter in a family with four sons.

The sons were adored; Anne was only tolerated. The sons attended college while Anne stayed home and ironed their shirts."

I could picture this clearly in my head—a young, dark-haired, thinner Anne, ironing with swift, hard strokes.

"No wonder Grandmother Anne and Aunt Beryl are so close," I said. "They're like identical twins, on the inside."

"No, you're wrong there. Anne is angry. Beryl is fearful. There's a bond between Beryl and Anne, but their pumps draw from different wells."

"What's Beryl so scared of?"

"I can't say for sure, though perhaps it stems from losing her parents at such a young age."

"But my mother was even younger. In fact, it's Aunt Beryl who can drive and my mother who can't."

"Don't you see?" Grandfather Mitchell ran his palms across the fringe of hair above his ears. "Loretta faces her fears. She understands that the loss of her parents has left her somewhat handicapped, if you'll excuse my use of the word. Beryl denies her pain and won't face it, so it catches up with her. Let's not underestimate the effects of her brief marriage, either. That dentist truly broke her spirit."

Grandfather Mitchell was really trying to explain it to me, but I needed more time, to explain it to myself. I stood up a moment—my legs and back tore away from the plastic with a *swerip* sound—and reached over to touch Grandfather Mitchell's wrist. It had pale brown spots. "You're so nice," I said. "Thanks so much for talking to me."

But he pulled his wrist away as if I'd burned him. "Don't thank me," he said, from the back of his throat, in a voice that sounded far away. "You have nothing to thank me for. I allowed Anne to . . . be herself." He cleared his throat, and the faraway voice vanished. "Still, parents shouldn't look back. Anne is always telling me this. We didn't do badly, did we? Your father's a fine man. Anne taught him to work hard, and to respect hard work, in himself and in others. Though perhaps it was a bit rougher on Robert than on most other children. Anne was so difficult, you see. She couldn't forgive her family for cheating her. But why look back? Robert couldn't have turned out better, not if we'd done our very best."

Hold the phone! I nearly said out loud, feeling about as dizzy as I had after taking Barry on the Tilt-A-Whirl. Grandfather Mitchell was smart enough to see through Grandmother Anne, but not strong enough to stand up to her. He felt sorry for her, but he knew she should have gotten over her anger a long time ago. He was ashamed of himself for standing by while Anne was a harsh mother to their son—but no harm done, because their son had turned out well.

Their son, my father. No wonder he'd wanted to live his life on a submarine! It was a chance to get away, far away, to a place nobody could visit or write to or call, a secret place, where nobody could ever find you, not an angry mother or a sweet, helpless father, a place that wasn't really a place at all, but a random, swirling path in the depths of the ocean.

We heard rustling from the bedroom. A moment later, Grandmother Anne emerged in a shapeless tan housedress with a buttoned-up collar. Her skin looked papery; her hair stuck to her head where a pillow had flattened it. She was suddenly looking very old. "This is a surprise," she said. "Old people don't like surprises. Why didn't you call first?"

"But, Grandma, you called my mother—for your prescription." I handed her the white bag.

She opened it and peeked inside. "Oh, yes," she said, crinkling the bag closed. "My vitamins."

I didn't dare say a word.

"Ellen's brought us some rye bread," Grandfather Mitchell said.

"Seedless, I hope? Old people shouldn't eat seeds. It interferes with their digestion."

This was new, calling herself old. I said, "Maybe you can pick them out."

Grandmother Anne's icy blue eyes studied me, this surprise visitor who had brought seeds into her home. "Now that you've had your visit with Mitchell, you may have your visit with me. In private." Grandfather Mitchell got up and said he wanted to watch television. But when he went into the bedroom, I didn't hear the TV click on.

This was their life together. My chest tightened; suddenly I felt like there wasn't enough air in this room.

Grandmother Anne sat down opposite me. "What did you and Mitchell have to say to each other?" she asked. "You must have done all the talking, since old peoples' lives are so monotonous."

"Well . . ." I decided to keep my visit with Grandfather Mitchell private too. "I told Grandpa about a boy I have a crush on. He's an identical twin. The problem is, he's going out with somebody else."

Grandmother Anne folded her hands—the hands that had ironed shirts for four brothers. "And what pearls of wisdom did Grandfather Mitchell bestow upon you? To pursue the other twin?"

"He told me, don't give up," I said. "He told me, wonderful things can happen."

Grandmother Anne crossed her thick legs. She wore slippers that were part white feathers, part bald, like half-plucked chickens. She's had a tough life, Grandfather Mitchell had said. And she taught my father the value of hard work. I decided to buy her a new pair of slippers on her next birthday. "And what else?" Grandmother Anne said.

"Nothing else, I said with a shrug.

Her eyes drooped into a squint. "Boy crazy, just like your mother. You're the image of Loretta, skimpy clothes and all. Boys—that's all she ever thought about."

I knew that wasn't true. Loretta had fallen in love with my father instantly. He'd been the only one. "You don't approve of my mother," I said, a little surprised to hear myself say it out loud.

"I have good reason not to," Grandmother Anne replied.

I leaned forward—*swerip*—resting my elbows on my knees. "Please tell me the good reason," I said.

Grandmother Anne inhaled deeply, and her exhale said, All right, you asked for it. "I suppose you're old enough to hear this," she said. "The full story of how I learned about your mother's use of illegal substances. Not long after Robert told me he intended to marry Loretta, I stopped by her apartment for a friendly chat. Her door was open. It was always open. Back then she called herself a free spirit, or some such nonsense, and didn't believe in locks. I found her lying on her couch, in a flimsy wisp of a nightgown, staring up at a bulb overhead. 'What is it, child?' I said. 'Aren't you feeling well?' Loretta muttered something about the colors and the patterns in the light. Naturally I became concerned, and sat down beside her. Do you know what she said to me then? This lovely, waiflike, golden-haired girl? She said, 'I'm wasted.' I had no idea what this meant, only that it was very horrible. Her sister, Beryl, explained it to me. So now you see, Ellen, why I don't approve of your mother."

I sat there, stunned. Not by the story, but by Grandmother Anne's horror, as fresh as the day this had happened, which must have been nearly twenty years ago.
"But it was so long ago," I said.

"Call me old-fashioned. If you were me, you wouldn't
want Loretta marrying your only child!"

If I were Grandmother Anne? How could I wish my
parents had never married—and wish myself and Barry out
of existence? "It was so long ago," I repeated.

Clearly my reaction was not what Grandmother Anne
had hoped for. She tightened her lips, and then said, "People don't change much, as you'll learn as you get older.
Basically Loretta is still an irresponsible teenager. Lord
knows I've tried, but there's no talking to her."

That was when I heard it—the jealousy in Grandmother
Anne's voice. My mother, a free spirit, no locks on her door.
To Anne, who'd had to iron shirts, it must have seemed like
Loretta was getting away with something, and was still now
somehow getting away with it.

There was definitely something wrong with the air in
here. "I really have to go," I said.

"Oh, must you?" Grandmother Anne said, but it sounded
like, yes, you must.

I went outside to the garden, and smiled at several old
ladies sitting peacefully on green benches, in the shade of
tall trees. They smiled back and said, "Hello, dear." There
was a slight breeze, and leaves rustled.

At dinner, Loretta asked me about my day. She was
feeding Barry some chicken and soft, cooked carrots, and
he was spitting out the carrots.

"It's Grandmother Anne," I said. "She's . . . she's
so . . ."

"Yes, she is!" Loretta laughed. "And she always has been!"

I laughed too. "She paid me a compliment, though I don't think she meant to. She said I was the image of you, when she first knew you."

"Thank heavens you're not!" Loretta said, trying again with the carrots. "I was wild back then. To be fair to Anne, I should say that she didn't have an easy time with me."

"What did Daddy think?" I couldn't imagine him approving of Loretta's behavior.

"Your father loved me," she said, smiling down at Barry. "He wasn't at all happy with what I was doing to myself, but he figured it was my way of dealing with the death of my parents. He was right. My parents were awfully strict, El, always punishing me and Beryl. Beryl was frightened of them, but I fought with them constantly. I guess I always figured I'd have lots of time to be nice to them later, when I was all grown up. But they died before we ever got to be friends. Anne never understood, though I tried many times to explain it to her."

There's no talking to her, Grandmother Anne had said. "So when exactly did you stop being so wild?" I asked her.

"Let's see," Loretta said. "I met Robert when I was nineteen. Not for about a year after that. Anne always exaggerated the time and the extent of it. When Robert and I got married, I was twenty-one, and the only chemicals in my system were entirely my own." She looked up at me, her gray blue eyes soft in the summer light. "Your father stood by me, though it meant defying his mother. It's wonderful, El, to be loved like that."

Robert had defied Grandmother Anne, which was a lot more than Grandfather Mitchell had ever done. Something swirled around in my chest, something bright and soft, like

217

the glow of candlelight. Defying Grandmother Anne must have been very hard. I bet he thought he wasn't even capable of it, until he stretched his abilities and made himself capable of it.

I hadn't felt this way in a long, long time—proud of my father.

Clearing the table, I noticed that the July page on the kitchen wall calendar didn't have my Barry schedule on it. "Look, Mom, you forgot," I said, pointing to the calendar. "Not that you need to write it down—my schedule is set in stone inside my head."

"Buhb," Barry said.

"That's 'bubbles,' " I told Loretta. "He wants to blow bubbles when he takes his bath."

Loretta gave me a world-weary look that meant, I knew that one, Ellen. "Why don't you forget the Barry schedule?" she said. "Use your own judgment with him from now on. And don't look so thrilled—I'll still be keeping an eagle eye on you. By the way, you got a letter from Roz. It's on your bureau."

I ran into my room and tore the envelope open.

> *Camp Pine Grove*
> *Moosehead Lake, Maine*
> *June 27*
>
> *Dear Ellie,*
> *Greetings from the top of the U.S.A.! So far, so good. We draw for hours every day, and swim every afternoon in a cold, blue lake. I'm in a log cabin surrounded by pine trees, with six other girls. They're mostly very nice, except for one girl who reminds me of Susie Brockleman. She's*

218

incredibly talented. How is it that some jerky people are loaded with talent? Maybe you can figure it out for me. The girl I like best, it turns out, has a sister who is deaf. Isn't that a coincidence? She's teaching me American Sign Language. Already I can say, I'm hungry, mad, tired, happy, sad, confused. So what else is there in life?

I met a guy here. His name is Jack. I'm almost in love. By the time you read this, I probably will be. He's got hazel eyes, and long brown hair (to his shoulders!) and a soft voice that is very sexy. Also he is smart. I know I'm lucky, you don't have to tell me.

Please say hi to your mother and to Barry. Write soon!

Love, Roz

P.S. I forgot to say, I've been thinking about something. You should add two more professions to the pie graph—Historian and Biographer. Because you like thinking about why things happen, and why people turn out the way they do.

P.P.S. Listen, write very soon! I miss you and all that.

So I added Historian and Biographer to the pie graph. Actually I liked both ideas—taking a good, hard look at whole periods of time, or at people's whole lives. I began spinning around the spinner. Explorer. Tap Dancer. Newscaster. Pediatrician. Construction Worker. Opera Singer.

Maybe I might even write a biography someday on the artist Roz Spinak and call it *Toy Wooden Soldiers*.

But it would have to wait until after the one on Barry.

15

"I have big, big news," Robert said excitedly. *It* was late afternoon on July 3, and Robert had just come home. "That job at CHINFO I applied for last year—it's all arranged. Starting in November, I won't be going up to Connecticut for my shore leave. I'll be here at home for two years."

"Sweetheart, that's great!" Loretta said. "I just knew you'd get it."

"November," I said. "That's four months away. That's a long time—I mean, that's a long time for you to be home. I mean, congratulations, I'm proud of you." Since visiting my grandparents, I'd been thinking about telling Robert I was proud of him, but this was the way it came out.

"Thank you," Robert said. "It makes me feel proud, to have you proud of me."

My face grew warm. Robert's cheeks turned a bit red. So when do you get old enough so you don't blush anymore?

I was grateful when Barry changed the subject. "Tull," he said.

Both Robert and Loretta looked at him.

"Barry wants to see his turtle," I said. I had to admit I still got a kick out of being the only person in the whole world to always understand Barry, now that Aunt Beryl had taken herself out of the running. I went into Barry's room to get the tank. So then for a while we all sat around the living room and watched the turtle splash about, slowly sweep his head from side to side, blink, turn around, and then tuck in his head and take a nap.

When the turtle went to sleep, Barry said a bunch of words that made me feel a sort of pinch in my heart. "No hurt," he said. "Safe, hard shell."

I knew my parents didn't understand the words. But for a moment I couldn't talk. I'd bought the turtle so Barry could feel comfortable watching another creature's slow-as-molasses movements. But I hadn't realized that Barry could know anything about his own defenselessness.

I translated what he'd said for my parents. "Barry," I added. "How about giving your turtle a name?"

"Mister Shell," he said quickly, and so clearly that everybody understood.

I offered to cook dinner—spaghetti and meatballs. It was mostly an excuse to go into the kitchen and think for a while. Except that I kept forgetting things I usually knew and had to go back to the living room all the time.

"Mom, where's the olive oil?"

"Where it always is, on the shelf over the sink."

"I can't find the Parmesan cheese."

"It's still in the refrigerator."

"What happened to the colander?"

"It's exactly where you put it, hanging over the stove— unless it ran away."

So maybe what was really happening was I was trying to get used to the idea of seeing Robert every night for two years, two whole years.

At dinner, Robert fed Barry, who twice used his spoon all by himself and clamped his mouth around it. But both times the spoon just stayed there and Robert had to take it out.

"You might not be the only one who's about to start a new job," Loretta told Robert. "Last night I tried to convince El to work part-time at the library this summer, as a page."

"What does that mean, a page?" Robert asked.

"It means filing cards into the card catalog," I answered. "And shelving books. And checking books in and out. It means working five days a week, four hours a day, for four dollars an hour. Plus there'll be several other kids my age working there."

"Why don't you do it?" Robert said. "It sounds good." And something about the way he said it—gentle, sensible, encouraging—made it actually sound pretty good.

"Okay," I said.

"Wonderful!" Loretta said. "You'll have lots of fun, you'll see."

After we finished the spaghetti and meatballs, I said, "I feel like going out for ice cream. Barry likes peach, I know that, and I want double chocolate. Mom, how about you?"

"Cherry vanilla," she said.

"That does it—three flavors to a quart." Suddenly I was blushing again. I'd completely forgotten Robert. "Oh, sorry," I said. "What do you want?"

"A little of each," he said easily. "I'll go with you, Ellen."

"You don't have to," I said, more out of habit than anything else.

"I'd like the air—and the company."

Outside, it was dark and cool and breezy, blowing my hair all around. Awnings flapped and made a loud slapping sound. Robert's hair blew forward too, and it looked better that way, not so severe.

"Which ice cream store do you prefer?" he asked me.

"There's a new place on Bleecker, called I Scream," I said. "I've only been there once, but it was so good."

"Do you like other flavors besides chocolate?" he asked.

"Not too much," I said.

"Are there any flavors you absolutely won't eat?"

"Yes. Mint." It felt a little like talking to a stranger. Except I noticed while he was talking that my head reached the top of his shirt collar, and not too long ago, my head only reached his shoulder. You can't notice something like that with a stranger.

As we turned a corner, we ran into Susie Brockleman. She was walking a big white poodle, and walking along beside her was a tall guy, with a long, glum face and a ponytail, who was *not* Ray Frost.

I felt absolutely thrilled. "Susie! How are you!" I cried.

"Fine," Susie said, with a suspicious frown. "We just saw each other at graduation, Ellen."

The dog barked, loud and hollow. It was shaved so weirdly it looked as if white pom-poms had been thrown at its head, ears, and legs—and stuck.

"Susie, this is my father, Robert Gray."

"Oh, hi," Susie said, now smiling sweetly.

"Pleased to meet you, Susie," Robert said. "That's a beautiful standard poodle. Do you show her?"

"Yes, Mr. Gray, Misty's won lots of prizes. Hey, you're the one on the submarine! Ellen gave a speech about you, sort of." Susie tossed her curls back, but the wind blew them forward again.

"So I guess it's all over between you and Ray Frost, right?" I said.

Susie bulged her brown eyes at me—an I-can't-believe-you-actually-said-that look. But then she sighed. "Yes, I'm afraid so. Stewart's much more my type. He writes poetry." Finally Stewart smiled. He had a gap between his front teeth.

I'll give Ray a call, I thought. I'll say, Let's put our two heads together, see what happens.

"Ellen, it was very upsetting," Susie pleaded. "Breaking it off with Ray."

Stewart stopped smiling. And I couldn't stop grinning a ridiculous big grin.

I Scream had a huge painting on the wall of a round screaming mouth with teeth like piano keys and a bright pink tongue. Robert and I stood beneath overly bright, glaring lights, behind a dozen people, waiting . . . and waiting . . . and waiting. The place was run on an assembly line, designed, I thought, for maximum slowness—one person took your order, another filled it, another handed it to you.

"Is that girl a good friend of yours?" Robert asked me.

"No, Susie Brockleman is nothing like my best friend, Roz." I noticed that Robert's eyes didn't look so icy or harsh. Was it because of the glaring lights, sort of canceling them out? He seemed on the whole much softer. "Roz is away for the summer," I said. "She's away at an art camp in Maine. I miss her."

"It's hard, isn't it, missing somebody? When I'm not here with you and Barry, I miss you both very much. And when I come back, you've changed so much in the meantime, I miss you all over again because I never got to see the changes when they happened."

Wait a minute. This didn't sound like Robert Gray, the man I'd always assumed saw the world only in logical, black-and-white terms. So how could he say things like this, things that came straight from his heart and went right into mine, and still do the kind of work he did? I thought I might never understand it. It's hard to wrap your mind around those gray areas, where good and bad things share the same space.

A woman in front of us ordered heavenly hash in a cup with mashed-up M&M's.

"What'll it be?" This came from a guy whose frizzy gold-brown hair was topped by a white cap with the round screaming mouth on it.

"Peach," I said. "Double chocolate. Cherry vanilla."

"Where do you want it, in your hand?"

"Not tonight. In a quart, please."

The guy scribbled it down on a pad. Then he turned to Robert. "What'll it be?"

"I'm with my daughter," Robert said, in an admiring tone I'd never heard from him before. Or else had never noticed. The I Scream guy was looking a little embarrassed about the way he'd spoken to me in front of my father.

We sat on round plastic stools that were way too small and way too low to the ground, while waiting for our order to be filled.

"I think you should know, I miss you too when you're away," I said.

"On the boat, we often talk about our teenage daughters," Robert said. "They seem to have an especially hard time of it—running away from home, trouble in school.

Basically the crew think it's because all teenage girls are crazy, mixed up. But I've been thinking, it might be that teenage girls are really almost young women, and all their feelings aren't sorted out yet, so when their fathers leave, they're not sure if their fathers are leaving because of them."

Wow, I thought. He's definitely changing. And it's not a trick of the lights. I heard patience, tolerance, and understanding in his voice. I knew it was because of Barry, because Barry could do that to you.

Robert swiveled around to face me, and his knees bumped into mine. "You see, don't you, Ellen, that I was never leaving to leave you?"

"Yes," I said.

The Fourth of July was a completely gorgeous night— mild and clear, with a bright, soft, purple sky. Loretta, Robert, Barry, and I were all up on the crowded roof of a building on the Bowery, waiting for a big fireworks display over the East River. You had to know someone to be invited to this roof, and a friend of Maribeth's lived in the building. The place was so packed, it looked as if all the people who lived here had told all their friends to invite all of their friends.

Maribeth wore a pale yellow dress that shone like moonlight. "Sam stayed home," she said. "He hates fireworks. Ellen, you're a knockout in that miniskirt. Hold on, I've got something for you." From a big shoulder bag, Maribeth pulled out a soft, floppy, plaid tennis hat.

"Oh, that's great," Loretta said. "It'll keep the sun off your head this summer."

But I knew what this gift was really all about. I remembered that afternoon in Maribeth's gallery, when she had told me that sadness that didn't go away could be worn like a plaid hat. "Thanks, Maribeth," I said, and gave her a hug. For the moment, I tucked the plaid hat under my arm.

When the fireworks began, Robert lifted Barry up onto his shoulders. Light and noise cracked open the night air, and the whole rooftop oohed and ahhed and clapped. I looked around at the other buildings nearby. All throughout the area, hundreds and maybe thousands of people were looking to the sky, their faces brightened by brilliant light.

A huge, glowing gray-and-white cloud of smoke drifted slowly over our heads, smoke from the fireworks that began to obscure our view. People groaned in disappointment.

"Nellie," Barry said. "Ooh, look. Big, pretty, cotton cloud." And he laughed and clapped his hands.

I translated Barry's words. He's got such an interesting mind, I thought. He likes smoke better than fireworks.

The smoke thickened and a lot of people started to leave. I took a look at my family. They weren't moving. Barry had his thin legs wrapped around Robert's neck, and Robert's strong grip held his ankles firmly. Loretta placed her hand on Robert's shoulder, and my parents looked at each other. "Let's stick around awhile," Loretta said.

I reached up to take hold of Barry's hand, small and damp. Then I put on my plaid hat and stood gazing up at the pretty smoke.